"I saw you in the rocks after you let the horse go."

"You could have killed us all with your rifle, but you spared our lives." She looked away from him as she finished her statement.

"But the other warriors would have killed me."

"The men of my village are fools!" she interrupted. "They are nothing but fools."

Sparks snapped in the girl's eyes. Nathan, a bit confused, asked, "And what about the women?"

"Squaws! They are all squaws."

"And . . . what about Tachechana?"

The girl sprang to her feet, knocking over the stool she had been sitting upon. Her hand went instinctively to the handle of the tomahawk in the thong that served as a belt to her loose fitting deerskin shirt. She paced to the wall away from the table, then came storming back.

"Tachechana is the daughter of Great Bear the Chief. There is no brave in our village that can ride like her, shoot like her, or fight like her. But, because she is not a man, she cannot be Tachechana. She must become a squaw! *I will die first!*"

Tachechana

JACK METZLER

Serenade/SuperSaga
BOOKS
of the Zondervan Publishing House
Grand Rapids, Michigan

A Note from the Author:
I love to hear from my readers! You may correspond with me by writing:
Jack Metzler
1415 Lake Drive, S.E.
Grand Rapids, MI 49506

ISBN 0-310-47511-2

Edited by Leonard E. LeSourd
Designed by Kim Koning

Printed in the United States of America

89   90   91   92 / 10   9   8   7   6   5

To Linda, who is the spirit of . . .
Tachechana

The White Man Has a Word

Chapter

1

INTO THE MOONLESS NIGHT they pursued him like hounds. Now Nathan Cooper knew his only chance for survival was to hole up and hope they overlooked him. But there was no hole. The deep prairie grass was not much to hide him from the keen eyes of the Sioux war party. All he could do was lie there smelling the dirt, the sweet grass, and the raw fear that seeped from his skin. Fear and he were old companions.

It had been about seven hours since Nathan first saw them as he crossed the ridge between the two river systems he had been trapping. For months now he knew the Indians were in the vicinity, but by carefully moving from one stream to the other he had been able to elude them. Today was different. Early in the day they struck his trail while they were hunting. Since food was plentiful and scalps were not, they began following him. About the time the old trapper, though not as old as he looked, spotted them on his trail, they also saw him. They, a hunting (war) party of about a dozen braves, were a long mile or so behind him.

At first he was not overly concerned, for the big horse he

straddled was more than a match for any Indian pony. His powerful animal was of chestnut color with three white stockings and a small white star between his eyes. More than once the stallion, blessed with both speed and endurance, had gotten the trapper out of trouble with Indians. With a comfortable lead, plus his good Henry repeating rifle, and the skills acquired through many years of hunting the forests and prairies, Nathan felt confident about his situation.

His first strategy was to put on a burst of speed to convince the Indians that their ponies had no chance against so fine a horse as his. He didn't even look back for the first two miles of open prairie, but when he did, his surprise was more than mild. One of the Sioux, by far the smallest warrior he had ever seen, had actually closed some of the gap between them. At first he thought the gain made by the Indian was because he was so small, but then he noticed that the horse he was riding was a marvelously proportioned animal. The trapper grinned tensely as he realized he was in for one tough race.

The rest of the war party, on their lesser mounts, were stretched out in a line behind the leader. Nathan knew only too well what a patient people the Sioux were.

Where did an Indian get a mount like that? thought Nathan, as he spurred his own horse on. *Some poor farmer probably lost his scalp trying to save that animal!*

Nathan had been trapping this area for almost a year and a half, so he had a slight advantage over the Indians. Their nomadic way of life had brought them here only a few months earlier. The area was an ideal place for a trapper. The west edge of his trap line was at the very foot of

Wyoming's Big Horn Mountains, and stretched east to the grassy plains and forested areas around Goose Creek and the feeder streams of what would someday be called Clear Creek. He sometimes got as far east as the Powder River. Normally the Sioux would be east of his domain, but the Indians claimed all they could hold in battle.

He was now riding his horse at almost top speed and swinging slightly to the north. He felt he could lose the Sioux in rocky hills he knew of to the north and west of Goose Creek. As he topped out on the first of the hills Nathan again looked back. The little Indian and his valiant mount pressed on.

"That savage must be the son of a great chief," muttered the trapper to himself, "to be so small and have a horse like that. Surely one of the older, stronger braves would take it from him if that were not the case. I give him credit though; he sticks to it like they were part of each other."

Immediately after putting the hill between himself and the Indians Nathan made a sharp turn to the north. If he could get to the forest and the rocky hills before the Sioux saw him, he might lose them where the tracking was much more difficult. The rocks would also be a good place to make a stand if it came to shooting.

Nathan hated the thought of shooting another human being. His upbringing as a young man back East revolted at the thought. Perhaps it was also fear. After all, had he not come West to prove to himself that he was no coward?

From childhood he remembered phrases like ". . . all men are created equal . . ." and ". . . the color of a man's skin is not the proof of the man."

It was true. He had met many red men who were more

noble than whites. And the few black people he had met, he liked. But these were Sioux and they were out to remove his hair. It was prematurely thin and gray, but he meant to keep it as long as possible. Furthermore, he was sure he was the only man with a gun.

Physically, Nathan was not a big man, standing about five feet ten inches in his Indian moccasins. His weight was about one hundred fifty-five pounds. There was not an ounce of fat on him, and he was far stronger than he looked for his forty-two years. Nor was he ashamed of his abilities as marksman or horseman.

As he came to a group of trees that would conceal his movement for a time, he decided to slow the Indians down by laying out some false tracks. He rode first one way, then the other, circled and dodged until he was sure the Sioux would be confused enough to give him time to make it to the rocks and the protection they offered. Then, again at top speed, he dashed out of the trees and headed for the rocks.

The safety of the rocks was only about one hundred yards off when Rowdy stumbled and nearly fell. Nathan was agonizingly aware that his horse was lame and his scalp in danger. He decided in an instant what he must do. Slowing his horse, he slipped the rifle from its scabbard, and as he came to the first large boulder, leaped onto it with an agility that belied his age. From stone to stone he sprang until he had a commanding view of the plain below him. He saw his riderless horse disappear into a ravine just as the small warrior on the Arabian burst from the forest. With a shrill war whoop he pointed his lance in the direction of Nathan's horse and urged the last reserve of speed from his own mount.

The route the Indians were taking would bring them within sixty or seventy yards of where the trapper lay in ambush. How easy it would be to pick them off one at a time as they rode by. Slowly he worked the lever of his rifle to chamber a cartridge.

As he brought the gun to his cheek, its sights fell on the body of the small savage. Ever so slowly he took up the slack in the trigger. Then his hand began to shake. He could not kill the small warrior, even though the Sioux would kill him if the tables were turned. Now they were all passing him by.

Why waste human life? he reasoned. But he knew the shaking of his hand and the terror in the pit of his stomach. He and fear had lived a long time together.

He lowered his gun and sat still for a few moments. He had to get his wits about him for the long walk back to his cabin. As the last Indian disappeared into the ravine, he scrambled over the rocky hill and onto the prairie in the direction of Goose Creek and the safety of his cabin. He was worried about Rowdy, his horse, but deep down he knew the animal would show up in a day or two.

Darkness was falling and Nathan breathed easier, knowing both he and his horse would now be much safer. Suddenly deeply fatigued, he sat down in the tall lush grass. He had rested about half an hour when his solitude was shattered by the snort of a horse. It wasn't Rowdy! Somehow the Indians had sorted out his deception and were once again on his trail.

An overcast sky meant it was going to be a velvety dark night. Nathan knew from stories that passed from campfire to campfire of the keen night vision of the Sioux; he was

13

not about to try anything foolish. Since he could not see them yet, he felt safe in assuming they could not see him. In a low crouch he scrambled toward a slight depression where the grass was taller and where he could hide and outwait the Indians.

In the blackness, he tripped over the carcass of an animal and pitched headlong in the dirt. Pain shot through his twisted knee. Even worse—the barrel of his rifle was jammed with dirt as he fell. Now, unhorsed, lame knee, and armed only with the knife and tomahawk in his belt, he must face a dozen of the pride of the Sioux nation.

As Nathan eased himself into the thickest patch of prairie he could find, he thought it funny that he should notice how sweet it smelled. *Nothing is sweet when you're close to death,* he thought. He was a fox. They were the hounds. *Will the fox outlast the hounds?* he wondered.

An hour passed, the Sioux were stretched out in a line, combing the prairie to find him. This sweep would take them to the south. Would they turn and make another pass? Dare he risk detection by moving? No! He must stay still and hope they missed him. His stiffened knee made it impossible to try any travel tonight.

Another hour passed before he heard the muffled steps of horses again. He pressed himself deeper into the moist prairie earth. This time an Indian passed on each side of him. He held his breath as long as he could. They had neither seen nor heard him.

Are they going to search all night for me? Nathan wondered. He already knew that was not the nature of a Sioux warrior, for a brave that dies in battle at night must forever ride the happy hunting ground in darkness.

Another hour passed and again he heard the terrifying steps of Indians' horses. One was closer this time. Now coming right at him. What to do? The horse stopped only a foot or so from Nathan's face. He turned and, in the dim light available, saw that the horse standing over him was the Arabian.

He was just about to climb to his feet when he felt the prod of a war lance laid lightly on his left shoulder. He waited. An eternity passed in a few seconds. Fear oozed freely from his pores.

Nathan bunched his muscles for a leap at the Indian when the lance was pressed harder on his shoulder—not to inflict pain, it appeared, but to hold him stationary while the Sioux decided what to do.

The silence was broken by an Indian at the far end of the line. "Is this white man a mole that can crawl under the grass and not be seen?"

Nathan, during his years in the foothills of the Rockies, had learned enough of the Sioux language to understand the words. One after another the red men complained that the trapper was some kind of an evil spirit to be able to avoid them. All the while the lance of the young warrior pressed him firmly into the dirt.

At last the council was ended. The hounds had given up. Ever so slowly the tip of the lance was withdrawn.

Am I dreaming? Is this savage going to let me go after all we have been through today? thought Nathan.

For a long moment the Indians sat astride their horses, saying nothing. Then, one at a time, they turned to retreat to their encampment. The smallest warrior was the last to go. As the Indian turned his horse, careful not to step on the trapper, Nathan looked up to see the face and form of his benefactor. He could not believe his eyes.

There, astride the finest war horse he had ever seen, complete with war paint and all the accouterments of a seasoned warrior, sat a girl!

Chapter
2

THE NEXT MORNING the Indian village was tense. Word of the trapper's escape had spread like fire from tepee to tepee. By sunrise the entire encampment was aware of the warriors' failure to capture their quarry.

The village itself was a collection of tepees located on the high bank of the river. Some of the tepees were decorated with designs; some had colorful pictures of hunting and battle scenes. In front of each was a holder for bow, arrows, and lances. On each lance hung the scalps of its owner's victims. Each tepee had at least one horse nearby; some had several. Since horses were a sign of wealth to the Sioux, each Indian warrior prided himself on the number and quality of his animals.

The squaws of the village were busy cooking, grinding meal, making clothing, or tending babies. Some of the lodges had more than one squaw of nearly the same age, as polygamy was commonly practiced by the Sioux. A great warrior or chief might have as many as three wives. Wives or squaws were considered servants of their husbands, to bear children and tend to every need of their man. This was the social stratum for all Sioux women, except one.

Tachechana was the only child of the Chief of this village. Her father, Great Bear, had only one wife, who had died giving life to Tachechana. While every young maiden in the tribe would have readily consented to be the Chief's mate, he chose to remain true to the wife of his youth. He raised his daughter by himself, a task that required all the wisdom the great Chief could muster. Because he did not know how to teach her to be a woman, he taught her to be a warrior instead. While the other girls of the tribe were learning to sew, she was learning how to throw a knife and a tomahawk. While others were learning to prepare food, she was learning the fine art of marksmanship with bow and arrow. While others were caring for younger brothers and sisters, she was caring for her father's horses.

Oh, how she loved horses! By the time she had passed her fifteenth winter, she was one of the three best riders in the village. It was during that fifteenth summer that her father killed a great Arapaho Chief and brought his horse back to the village as a prize of battle. Tachechana took one look at that Arabian beauty and fell in love with it. The Chief, being no match for the pleading look in his daughter's eyes, announced that the horse was to be the exclusive property of Tachechana. Anyone who dared try to take it from her would face the wrath of the great Chief himself.

An anguished cry had gone up from the braves. It was bad enough to give a female a horse, but to give her one on which she could outrun every man of the tribe, including her own father, was more than their pride could tolerate. Many a council fire burned while debate raged among the warriors and elders over the "problem" of a squaw with a horse. Each time Great Bear would end the debate with the declaration that he was Chief. He had won the horse in battle. It was his privilege to give the horse to whomever he chose, and he chose to give it to his daughter. He would then leave the council fire and the debate was over.

Because of the great speed and free, flowing beauty of the horse, she named it "The Fox."

Three summers later the braves were still after the horse. Some had proposed marriage to get the Arabian. Tachechana would have none of them. Whenever one of the braves would suggest matrimony, she would whip out her tomahawk and inform the suitor that if he beat her in a battle to the death he could have what was left of her. Some would have accepted this challenge to get that horse, except for the stern warning of the Chief ringing in their ears.

So it was that Tachechana began to ride, first with the hunting parties then with the war parties. She had never killed a man in battle, but she had earned two eagle feathers for being the first to touch the enemy, preferring the thrill of battle to its bloodshed.

She could not explain to herself why she spared the white man. Since she had led the chase, the failure would be placed on her. She ignored the taunts of the male warriors, but her father, being Chief, had to listen. By tribal law the braves could call a council to determine if the shame of last night was the fault of Tachechana. Great Bear had no choice. Tonight there would be a council fire and the question of the girl's right to ride with the braves would be decided.

The air remained unexplainably charged all day as

preparation for the council was made. Even the children could feel the tension. Their play was strangely silent. The squaws, who now were extremely jealous of Tachechana, were smiling among themselves and thinking that this time the spoiled daughter of the Chief would be brought down to their level. The old men, called Elders or Gray Heads, sat and contemplated the coming meeting and asked the "Great Spirit" or "Giver of Life" to help them in their deliberations. Their opinion would be the determining factor at the council.

Finally the sun touched the western horizon and the council fire was lit in front of the tepee of Great Bear. The Indians gathered around the fire according to their social status. At the outermost fringe of the circle sat the squaws and their mostly naked children. Inside that ring sat the young warriors who were not permitted to speak before the council. Closer to the fire were the braves, who because of their deeds in battle and hunting were permitted to address the Chief and Elders. Closer still to the fire were the Elders.

The last to appear was Great Bear himself. He stood there for a period of time, arms folded across his chest, his six foot stature tall for an Indian, his long flowing headdress of many feathers trailed down his back. In his right hand was the great peace pipe of his village.

Silence fell over the entire assembly. When the Chief had the attention of everyone, he glided rather than walked to the fire, picked up a slender switch of wood and thrust one end of it into the fire. When it was well-ignited, he pulled it from the fire and lit the tobacco in the pipe. Then he took a long draft on the pipe, lifted it above his head, and blew the smoke skyward. Still standing, he gave the pipe to the Elder seated on his right, who took a long draft and blew the smoke toward the sky. Thus the pipe was passed around the circle of Elders and handed back to the Chief, who took its long stem and drove the tomahawk-like projection opposite the bowl sharply into the hardened earth.

"Let the council begin," he said and sat down.

At first there was a long silence, as each of the braves was a bit intimidated by the solemnity with which the council was begun. Finally a brave, tall and muscular for an Indian, sprang to his feet. There was a vivid scar on his right cheek and the top of his right ear was missing, the result of an encounter with a soldier's bullet.

"Let the council of the Sioux hear the words of Running Coyote. Has not my lance the scalps of ten Arapaho dogs hanging on it? Has not my bow brought many buffalo to the cooking pots of the village? Let the council of wise Elders hear me!"

"Speak Running Coyote," replied the Chief with a nod of his head.

"Our Chief is an owl, for he is the wisest of all the Chiefs of the Sioux. Yet he does not see the folly of having a squaw ride in the company of warriors."

Tachechana, seated with the young warriors, bristled at the word "squaw" and slammed her hand onto the ground. Ignoring her, Running Coyote, with doglike cunning, gave a detailed account of what had happened the previous night. "Had not the squaw, Tachechana, been there, the Giver of Life would have smiled on us and we would have rid our land of another of the white men," he concluded, the scar on his cheek glowing in the firelight.

Another arose with birdlike grace. "Let the council of the Sioux hear the words of Eagle Feather. See on my lance the scalps of seven Arapahos and two white soldiers. Was I not like the wind on the day we defeated the pony soldiers where the two rivers meet? Does not my arm draw the stiffest bow among us?"

"Speak, Eagle Feather," said Great Bear.

"Our Chief is an eagle that can see all things. He can see truth and justice as well as he can see a buffalo and a bear. Is it a good thing for warriors to follow a woman into battle? Yet there is not a horse between the Father of Rivers and the Great Mountains that can stay ahead of Tachechana's horse. In every battle she leads the true warriors of the Sioux instead of staying at the village to prepare food and make the tepee of her husband happy. I, Eagle Feather, ask that Tachechana be given to me for a wife. Then she would learn the rightful place of a woman."

A slender brave got up with a quick, nervous jump.

"Let the council of the Sioux hear the words of Swimming Otter. See the scalp of an Arapaho chief on my lance. Is not my lodge covered with the scalps of our enemies?"

"Speak, Swimming Otter."

"If the daughter of Chief Great Bear is permitted to ride with the warriors, it will not be long before all squaws will want to. . . . My own sister is asking for a horse of her own."

A murmur of assent flashed around the circle of warriors. The gray-headed Elders shook their heads.

"Are our warriors dogs, that their women should scold them? Let Tachechana marry me or one of the other men of the village and learn the woman's place."

22

The murmur became a roar. One after another the braves spoke concerning Tachechana. Several asked for her as a bride that they might teach her what the Giver of Life had made her to be.

Throughout the council the Elders were silent, nor did Great Bear speak other than to acknowledge the right of each of the braves to do so without interruption. When the warriors had all spoken, the leaders sat for a period of time in contemplation. The wisest of the old men cleared his throat.

"Tachechana rides as well as any of the warriors of the Sioux," the ancient patriarch began. "Her arrow is always true to the mark. Yet, to have a woman lead the warriors in the hunt or the battle is not a good thing. The Arapaho will think we are weak if we send squaws into battle. Let the maiden be married!"

One after another the Gray Heads voiced their opinion that it was not right for a woman to do the things that the Chief's daughter was permitted to do. As Tachechana listened to these words, she became so angry her pulse pounded in her ears, and it seemed louder to her than dancing drums. She wanted to jump up and challenge each of them to a fight. Her hand nervously grasped and released the handle of the tomahawk she always wore in her belt. She thought them all to be fools, but she knew it would not be tolerated if she should speak to the council, especially now that the Elders had begun to pass their judgment. She sat in her place and looked at no one but her father.

Great Bear sat like a statue. Only his eyes moved as he listened to the arguments. His visage was stern, yet he showed no hint of his feelings as he listened. There was a long period of silence after the last of the Elders had spoken. Finally, Great Bear rose to his feet.

Now, thought Tachechana, *they will hear the words of their Chief and be silenced. He will tell them how wrong they are.*

Great Bear appeared truly magnificent as he stood there before his people. His headdress had more feathers in it than that of any other Chief they could remember. His muscles rippled beneath his deerskin shirt and breeches. His dark eyes seemed to penetrate the very souls of his people.

"The fathers of the Sioux are foxes," he began. "They see and know many things. They must know that Tachechana, the daughter of Great Bear, is inferior to none of the warriors of this village. She has proven her skill with the knife and the tomahawk. Her arrows always fly true. . . . Still, it is not good for a woman to lead a man. It is not good that the village of the Sioux be in turmoil because of one woman even though she be the daughter of the Chief."

Tachechana was shocked! Was this her father speaking? How could he betray her like this?

"She is a strong woman," continued the Chief, "and old enough to be the wife of a Sioux warrior. Those braves seeking to marry Tachechana must be at the tepee of Great Bear when the sun is at its highest tomorrow."

Having so spoken, he reached down for the pipe at his feet, turned on his heel and entered his tepee. The council was ended.

Chapter
3

THE FLAP THAT WAS THE DOOR of Great Bear's tepee had not stopped moving from his entrance when it was nearly torn off by Tachechana as she burst into his presence. It was not the "Skipping Fawn" as her name implied, but a "Spitting Wildcat" that entered.

For a long moment father and daughter stood looking at each other. Sparks snapped from the girl's eyes. The eyes of Great Bear showed concern and compassion. The girl was the first to speak.

"Why does the great Chief of the Sioux hate his daughter so much as to give her and her horse to a man against her will?"

"Be calm, my daughter," replied Great Bear.

"How can I be calm, when my father has turned his back on me?"

"I have not, nor will I," returned the Chief. "If my daughter will listen I will speak."

"But you have invited braves to come seeking a wife," ranted the girl.

"I asked that those seeking to marry Tachechana should come, but I did not say she would marry one of them," said Great Bear.

"But how—·"

"Be silent, my child, and I shall speak."

"Speak, my father," answered Tachechana in a more subdued tone.

"The heart of Great Bear is a turtle that plods slowly through the mud," began the Chief. "There is no daughter in the entire Sioux nation that is more honored by her father than Tachechana. Yet he is a Chief and must care for all his people. What the Elders have spoken at the council fire is true. My village is in turmoil because the Chief so honors his daughter. If Great Bear is to be a good Chief, he must consider what is best for all the people of the village.

"There is much of your mother in you." This was the first time she had ever heard Great Bear speak of his wife. Tachechana wanted to stop him and make him tell her more about her mother, but she knew she must not, for it brought pain to the Chief's eyes. "She, too, had a mind that would travel only one trail. I know it is not in the heart of Tachechana to marry and be as the squaws of the village, but the village will not be a happy one until she does, or . . . she leaves."

The silence following that statement was like that of a forest just before a storm. Tachechana tried to comprehend what her father was saying.

"What does my father mean?"

The Chief swallowed hard and said, "When the sun rises tomorrow you must take your weapons, food, and your horse and leave the village of Great Bear."

He paused to control his voice. "When the sun reaches the top of its circle, and those seeking a wife come, I will speak. I will tell them I have sent you away and the one

26

who brings you back unharmed shall have you as his wife. The only way you may return is with a husband."

The Chief turned from his daughter, not wishing to see the pain in her eyes, nor expose the pain in his own. Neither of them spoke for a long time. Tachechana was suddenly aware of how difficult this was for her father. She also saw a chance for a new adventure, and perhaps a way to win her cause before the eyes of her village. They both knew no brave of the village could bring her back unharmed if she didn't wish it. She was too much of a warrior for that.

"My father has spoken of the mother of Tachechana. Does the daughter have a right to know more of her mother?" questioned the girl.

"A cold wind blows in the chest of Great Bear whenever he thinks of his wife," began the Chief. "She was not a Sioux. She was not even an Indian. The mother of Tachechana was a white woman we captured when I led the braves against a wagon train. I found her lying in the grass. At first I thought she was dead, but when I touched her she rose to her feet. She showed no fear, nor did she cry out. She stood tall and proud as a Sioux woman would, and her eyes looked into my heart. Her eyes were the color of the underside of an aspen leaf early in spring, just like yours. Her manner was such that all the braves admired her and none would harm her."

The Chief paused for a long time. At length he cleared his throat and continued. "We did not drag her back to the village as we would any other captive, but caught one of the wagon train horses and she rode back to the village at my side. As we entered the village the squaws began to make sport of her, but when they saw the resolve in her eyes and the pride in the way she held herself they soon left her alone.

"I took her to my lodge which she immediately took over and made me understand I could not stay there. For a while Great Bear was the joke of the village. I brought her food, which she prepared for herself. I brought her the skins of deer, and she made clothes for herself. For the entire winter I lived in the tepee of my father.

"One spring day, as I brought her venison to eat, she asked me to stay and eat with her. She had learned our language, and many of our customs. She was becoming a Sioux. The heart of Great Bear was an eagle that soared over the highest mountains and spoke to the clouds each time we sat together to eat and talk. When the leaves fell from the trees that year I asked Green Eyes to be my wife. She agreed and we danced the wedding dance under the full moon."

Again the Chief was silent. Tachechana broke his reverie by touching him tenderly on the shoulder.

"That winter was one of great happiness. There was much food, and many beaver in the rivers and streams. Green Eyes went with me to trap the beaver, and she helped skin and stretch the hides. But I would not let her go with me to the trader for fear she would want to stay with the white man.

"She once followed me to the trader and walked up to him while we were trading. As I said before, she had a mind that would travel only one trail. The white man spoke to her in his own tongue, but she would only speak to him in Sioux. On the way back to the village I asked her why she did this and she said, 'The woman who is to give life to the child of a Sioux Chief should be a Sioux.' I knew then that Green Eyes would be my wife forever." Pride sparkled in the Chief's eyes.

"Through the spring and summer we had great happiness. We would ride out on the prairie and let the wind sing in our ears. We would lie on the floor of the forest and watch the trees dance to the song of the wind. We would splash in the streams, and we would laugh. . . ." The Chief's voice trailed off as he thought of the joy he had with his young wife, and how empty his life was without her.

"I do not wish to bring sorrow to the heart of my father," said Tachechana. But the Chief stopped her by holding up his hand.

"It is right that a daughter should know of her mother," continued Great Bear. "When she could no longer ride because she was with child, we stayed around the village. We would walk out on the prairie at night and watch the stars. She would try to teach me the white man's names for them. I would make fun of the names and we would laugh. We laughed much together. She would make signs in the dirt and tell me they were 'words.' She wanted me to learn to read the words so I could be a greater Chief, but I would only look into her sparkling eyes and laugh. . . . And she would go like this,"—he put out his lower lip like a pouting child and puffed out a little air—"and we both would laugh.

"Then, as the snow began to fly, and a new winter began, Green Eyes laughed less and less. She always had a smile for me, but I could see pain in her eyes. One night she told me the Giver of Life was about to give us a child. She called the Giver of Life 'God.' For two days the child fought to stay in the safety of its mother, but finally a girl child was born. Green Eyes said, 'Her name shall be Tachechana, the Skipping Fawn.'

"For the next few days Green Eyes lay on her blanket. She cared for you as best she could, but the Giver of Life took her spirit to the other world where she waits for Great Bear."

Tachechana felt a strange constriction in her throat. Her eyes stung, and for a moment she was afraid she was going to shed tears. Finally, her Indian nature took over and she regained control. It would never do for a warrior to cry. If she permitted herself to cry she would be acknowledging that she was no different than the other women of the village.

Her father had regained his composure. "I regret I did not learn the 'marks' in the earth that Green Eyes tried to teach me. Perhaps," he suggested, "Tachechana could do her people good by learning 'words,' as Green Eyes had called them. She could then come back and teach her people more of the white man's ways and maybe, just maybe, there would be peace."

"How can there be peace," asked the girl, "when the white man wants only to steal our land, and make the Sioux his slaves?"

"Are all men of the Sioux the same?" replied Great Bear. "All are strong and brave, but are there not some who speak two tales, and steal from their brothers? Among the Sioux there are good men and bad. So it is with the white man. It is sad that most white men we have seen are evil, but there are those who would be brothers to the Sioux. You must find such a man and learn of him the ways of the white man and teach him the ways of the Sioux."

"How will I be able to know such a man?"

"It will not be a simple task," the Chief replied. "But you are a bright girl. You have the understanding of your mother and the instincts of your father. With the help of the Giver of Life you will find such a man."

"Can a trapper be such a man?"

"Some trappers are good men."

"But they steal the beaver of the Sioux."

"Did the Great Spirit make the beaver for the Sioux only or for all men?"

"Is that why my father did not ride with the braves yesterday when they sought the trapper?"

"The paths of the old man and Great Bear have crossed many times. He did me no wrong."

"My father . . ." The girl hesitated.

"Speak my daughter."

"It is true that this Gray Head lives today because of me. When we were chasing him, his horse became lame. Rather than ride the horse to death, he jumped off and hid in the rocks towards the rising sun. I led the braves after the horse without a rider. When we were all out on the prairie I saw the Gray Head in the rocks with a rifle. He could have killed us all, but when he saw we were going past, he let us go."

She then related the story of the search that followed and of her finding him and not killing him.

"Did the daughter of the Chief do wrong to spare the life of one so brave?" she asked.

"All Sioux admire a brave man."

"But Running Coyote would have killed him."

"Running Coyote would kill anyone if it would bring him the praise of others."

"There is much I do not understand," concluded the girl.

"Running Coyote would steal from his brother, lie to his father, and even try to kill me and become Chief. But he is also a coward who is afraid of the price he might have to pay. He is an evil man. You must beware of him."

"Is it not better to trust him than a white man?"

"It is better not to trust Running Coyote at all," was the Chief's reply.

The next hour Tachechana readied herself for the biggest adventure of her young life. She gathered up her weapons and clothes, then put jerky and pemmican in small bags along with some parched corn and tied them in a bundle. After checking and rechecking her supplies she was ready for sleep. Before she crawled into her blanket, however, she went to the stream and drank until she could drink no more. She wanted to be sure to wake up early and her bladder was the best alarm clock on the prairie.

When she lay down, sleep was slow in coming. Her mind raced from thought to thought. First to the old trapper and the events of the previous day, then to the bittersweet story of her mother, then to the journey before her. Finally, she dozed.

It was still dark when she awoke. Quietly she stalked from the tepee and led her horse "Fox" to the front of the lodge. All was quiet in the village as she entered the tepee to gather her belongings. Just as she was about to leave her father sat up.

"Would the daughter of Great Bear leave her father without a farewell?"

This was the moment Tachechana dreaded. She had hoped Great Bear would remain asleep, unaware that her father had not slept all night. Now, with true Indian stoicism, he sat cross legged, back straight as one of his arrows. She walked in front of him and kneeled, head bowed to hide the hurt in her eyes. Great Bear placed his right hand on her head and took her right hand in his left. They remained that way in silence several seconds before Great Bear spoke.

"If the Sioux ever have a woman for a Chief, it will be Tachechana," he said.

His right hand, as gentle as thistledown, slowly slid down her face, over her cheek and under her chin. He elevated her head until she could no longer avoid eye contact. When she looked directly into his eyes he said, "The white man has a word called 'love.' Great Bear almost learned the meaning of this word from your mother. You must learn it, and bring back its meaning to the Sioux. Then we may be able to live together, red man with red man, red man with white man. You must learn what Green Eyes almost taught me."

Without a further word, his hands left his daughter, his arms crossed his chest, and he looked beyond the walls of his tepee into the darkness of the outside world. Tachechana arose, gathered the last of her belongings and stepped out into the gray dawn. With slow tread she led Fox through the village to the east. A ways past the last tepee she grabbed a handful of mane and threw herself onto the horse's back.

Slowly they moved down the bank, into the cold water and swift current of the river. When she had crossed the river and gained the east bank she turned and looked back at the village and the tepee of her father. There was no sign of life, yet she continued to look and memorized every line in the village that used to be her home. Sure at last that she would never forget one detail, she turned the horse eastward again into the dazzling light of the new sunrise.

Marks in the Earth

Chapter
4

THREE FULL DAYS HAD PASSED since the night of Nathan Cooper's ordeal. Now, as sunrise was starting a fourth day, he was beginning to feel concern for Rowdy, his horse. The big mountain-bred stallion should have found his way home by now. Perhaps he was now the proud possession of one of the Indians; if so, Nathan would be doing a lot of walking. He began to look at his options.

He could take all the beaver hides he could carry and strike out for the trading post on foot, though his twisted knee made walking painful. Once there he could trade for a horse, but it would not be a good one for so few skins. Or, he could try to catch a wild horse. One man on foot would have his hands full with a job like that. Or, he could walk back to where he left the horse and try to track him down. Again, a sizable job for a man on foot. One thing was certain, he had to get a horse under him again.

Nathan had just finished his breakfast when he heard a horse nicker. But it wasn't Rowdy. He sprang from the bench, a tingle of fear shooting through his stomach, and snatched up his rifle. If the Sioux had finally tracked him down, they were in for a fight before they hung his scalp on a lance! He knew no arrow could pierce the door of his shack, for it was made of oak planks he salvaged from the bottom of an abandoned wagon. His cabin was nestled between a horse shed on one side and a rock wall on the other. Attack was only possible from the front. Nathan knew he had food, water, and ammunition enough to hold off a major siege. He squinted out through a hole in the door carved out to accommodate a rifle barrel. What he saw stunned him.

Seventy-five yards out from his door stood his own horse. Directly behind the stallion was the girl warrior astride the Arabian. She sat there staring at the cabin door. Nathan carefully scanned every rock and tree to find the other braves, but soon convinced himself that she was alone. Slowly he opened the door and stepped out, rifle in hand, but not pointed at the Sioux. As he came out, the girl warrior sat straighter on the back of her mount and studied him. He returned her gaze. For a long time neither said a word. Finally, Nathan broke the silence, speaking in the Sioux language.

"Does the warrior of the Sioux come in peace?"

The girl replied by lowering the tip of her lance toward the ground. Nathan leaned his rifle against the frame of the door. He raised his right hand slowly, showing the girl his open palm and said, "The warrior of the Sioux is welcome if that warrior comes in peace."

Tachechana drove the tip of her war lance into the ground and raised her right hand. She barely touched the side of her horse with her heel, the mare started walking slowly past Rowdy and to within twenty-five yards of the trapper and stopped again.

"Why does a warrior of the Sioux honor a white man with a visit?" asked Nathan.

"I have come to return a horse to its owner," replied the girl in a voice she meant to be deep, but which came out sounding very much like the voice of a girl.

Nathan walked out to the front of the girl's horse and looked up into her face. "Does the Sioux always wear the paint of war when making a gift?" he asked.

She seemed confused by this question. Perhaps she had hoped to impress the trapper. "The war paint is for the Arapaho dogs that would steal such a horse," she said uncertainly.

To ease the tension Nathan said, "The gift of such a horse as this must be repaid. Will the warrior of the Sioux eat at the fire of a white man?"

The girl leaned forward and handed the reins of Rowdy to the trapper. He took them and led the horse into the small corral that was the animal's home. He turned to find himself face to face with the girl warrior. She had already slipped off her horse after leading the Arabian to the gate of the corral.

The girl was even smaller than she seemed while sitting astride her horse. Nathan studied her as much as he dared without offending her. If he held his arm out straight from his shoulder, she could walk under it without bowing her head. Though slight in body weight, she was well-muscled. The yellow and black chevron of war paint that apexed on the bridge of her nose drew Nathan's attention to her eyes, which were like no Indian eyes he had ever seen. Instead of steely black, hers were a pale green that you might look into, but not at, because of the illusion of transparency.

39

Tachechana was obviously uneasy under the trapper's scrutiny. "Where is the food of the Gray Head?" she asked. Nathan pointed to the cabin door with a smile.

Am I that old, at forty-two? he asked himself. *Maybe my gray head is not worth scalping then.*

"The warrior of the Sioux is welcome to all that I have," he said aloud.

Nathan wanted to take his rifle inside with him as he walked through the door, but he didn't because it might seem like an act of hostility. The girl's eyes missed nothing.

Inside the cabin she showed a lively interest in every detail. Directly opposite the only door was a boxlike cabinet on which sat a pail of water and a blue enameled basin. Under the cabinet were boxes and tins that contained food. To the right of the cabinet was a small stove with a steaming kettle on the back edge. Pots and pans hung on pegs around the stove. To the left of the cabinet were shelves that contained more boxes and tins, and next to the shelves was a doorway with no door that led to another room.

On the left wall was an old rifle that Nathan had retired when he got his new Henry. Shelves on that wall contained bullet molds, a powder keg and horn, other paraphernalia, and about twenty-five books. In the left corner near the door was a cot with blankets tossed helter-skelter from the previous night's sleep.

Against the right wall was a table, bench, and small stool. In the near right corner was a chest of drawers salvaged from the remains of a burned out wagon train. Most of Nathan's possessions had been gained that way.

"Does the Sioux warrior have a name?" Nathan asked.

"My name is Tachechana," she replied.

"It is a good name," he said, "but it is not a name for a warrior."

"The name was given to me by my mother." Her voice was almost apologetic, but her chin raised a little higher as she said it.

"It is a good name," he repeated as he put two chipped cups and bowls on the table. "I hope Tachechana likes the food of a 'Gray Head,'" he said with a smile.

He took the kettle from the back of the stove and poured a black liquid from it into the cups. Venison sizzled in the frying pan as he carved four slices from an oversized loaf of bread he had baked just yesterday. He motioned for the girl to sit down as he put a slab of meat in each bowl and two slices of bread beside it.

She sat on the stool and he on the bench on the opposite side of the table. She watched closely as he picked up the fork in one hand and knife in the other and cut a morsel from the meat in his bowl. She tried to imitate him, but had an embarrassing amount of trouble getting the fork to do what she wanted it to. As Nathan broke off a piece of his bread and dipped it into the meat juices he saw her problem. She was evidently very hungry, but wanted to imitate him.

Without looking at her, he took up the meat in his fingers. He then took a bite of meat and a bite of bread. Tachechana did the same and had no trouble in making the food disappear. Nathan turned his head so that his grin wouldn't be visible to his guest.

When Nathan took a sip of his coffee, the girl did too. Her mouth puckered and she seemed about to spit out the liquid. Somehow she was able to swallow it and even drank slowly, all that was in her cup. However, when Nathan got up for a refill, she put her hand over her cup so he could not refill it.

She looked surprised at the moist and light taste and texture of his bread, and Nathan realized that it was not hot and dry like the bread the Indians baked over their open fires. After finishing what had been placed in front of her, she looked over to the cupboard where the rest of the loaf sat. Nathan noticed the look in her eyes and cut another slice, dipped it in the grease and juices of the frying pan and put it in her bowl. It disappeared as had the previous two.

"Why did you bring my horse back to me?" asked the trapper.

"You are good to your horse," she replied.

"Why do you say that?"

"When we were chasing you, your horse went lame. You could have run him more and hurt him, but you didn't. You took a great risk, to protect your horse. Such a man and horse deserve each other."

Nathan realized for the first time that never at any point in the chase had he had the little warrior fooled. "And why did you spare my life when you found me on the prairie?"

"I saw you in the rocks after you let the horse go. You could have killed us all with your rifle, but you spared our lives." She looked away from him as she finished her statement.

"But the other warriors would have killed me—"

"The men of my village are fools!" she interrupted. "They are nothing but fools."

Sparks snapped in the girl's eyes. Nathan, a bit confused, asked, "And what about the women?"

"Squaws. They are all squaws."

"And . . . what about Tachechana?"

The girl sprang to her feet, knocking over the stool she had been sitting upon. Her hand went instinctively to the handle of the tomahawk in the thong that served as a belt to her loose-fitting deerskin shirt. She paced to the wall away from the table, then came storming back.

"Tachechana is the daughter of Great Bear the Chief. There is no brave in our village that can ride like her, shoot like her, or fight like her. But, because she is not a man, she cannot be Tachechana. She must become a squaw!"

She spat on the floor to get the taste of that last sentence out of her mouth. "Now, the only way I am welcome in my own village is to become a squaw. I will die first." And with that she drove the head of her tomahawk into the oak plank that was Nathan's table.

Nathan took another sip of his coffee and sat back to see what would happen next. The girl yanked the "hawk" from the table and stalked to the other side of the cabin. For a moment she stood looking at the books on the wall, and then sat down on the bed and looked back at Nathan. After several minutes of awkward silence he said, "What will Tachechana do now?"

A cloud of darkness drifted over the girl's eyes. Nathan was silent as he watched her contemplate that question.

"Do you know the marks in the ground?" she asked.

"I can track most animals," Nathan replied.

"No, I mean the marks that talk," continued the girl.

"I don't know what you mean."

43

"White men call them words."

"Oh," chuckled the trapper. "Yes, I can read."

"Can a Sioux learn to read?"

"Yes."

The girl jumped from the bed and flew to the table. She sat the prostrate stool back on its legs, looked Nathan in the eye, and said, "You teach Tachechana to read."

"It takes a long time to learn to read," explained Nathan.

"How long?"

"Many moons."

"I will learn!"

"But ... but ..."

"I *will* learn!"

"Where will you live while you learn?"

"Here."

Nathan had no intention of becoming a "squawman," especially with a Chief's daughter, whose father might at any moment have a change of heart and come riding in with his braves like a prairie blizzard.

"You cannot stay here," protested Nathan.

"Why?"

"Because you are a woman and I am a man."

"I know that," she pressed her advantage as sparks crackled in her eyes.

"It is not right for a man and a woman to live in the same house unless they are married."

"Then I will live outside with my horse."

"But the snows will soon come."

"Then I will build a tepee."

"I cannot allow a tepee here. It would draw other Indians to the place and I would soon lose my hair."

Tachechana nodded at the truth of his statement, but she pressed her attack. "If I were a man would you teach me?"

"Well, yes, but—"

"Then you are no different than the men of my village."

Nathan had never heard her father say his daughter had a mind that would travel only one trail, but he was quickly finding the truth of that statement. The thought of teaching the girl intrigued him. What to do? Dare he let her stay in the little fur-room shed built on the back of the cabin? What would any visiting trapper think or say? Of course he had never had a visitor in the year and a half he lived there. Yet, the propriety of having a girl in his cabin . . . Why, if word got out . . . But who would hear it?

Thoughts bordering on panic raced through his head. He really didn't want the girl to go, but he didn't want her to stay. The girl seemed to sense his mental anguish and a small smile cracked her face.

She's an Indian, and I'm white, thought Nathan. *She's female and I'm male. She's young and I'm getting old. She's heathen and I'm Christian. It just isn't right.*

But Nathan thought also of all the times he found himself talking to himself just to hear a human voice. He thought of how noble it would be to teach a Sioux to read. Surely, he knew, their relationship would only be that of mentor and student. He would not turn her away if she were a boy.

"I suppose I could make space for you in the fur shed," he said as he nodded toward the open doorway of the dark room.

As he rose and started toward the door, she sprang to her feet. A breeze of happiness blew the clouds from her green eyes. She stalked into the darkness behind him, blinked at the light that flooded the small room as he opened the shutters. In one corner was a pile of steel traps. Along both walls and on hooks in the ceiling hung upwards of one hundred prime beaver pelts still stretched on the willow hoops that gave them their round shape.

"We'll have to move the furs and traps out to the horse shed, and fix you up with some kind of a bed," Nathan said aloud, thinking that the rest of the cabin would certainly smell the better for it. Tachechana's face beamed.

The rest of the day was spent preparing the small room for the girl. Furs, traps, snares, and tools were all removed to the horse shed, which was already too small for the extra horse, but Nathan made room for them. While Tachechana swept out the room, he cut two poles about five feet long, and two more six and a half feet long. These he notched to form a rectangle about four by six feet. With the girl watching closely, he spiked the poles together at the notches and began to weave a rope spring across the frame. That completed, he reached up into the rafters of the cabin and brought down a mattress ticking. This he took to the edge of the forest, where he filled it with soft grasses and the tenderest ends of the balsam boughs. When the pole bed was in place in the shed room he smoothed out the mattress on the frame and told Tachechana to put her blankets on it. While she was getting her things from her horse, Nathan moved a box into the room, as a nightstand, and put a crude candle holder on it. A blanket was hung in the doorway to afford a measure of privacy.

By the time Tachechana finished arranging her belongings, Nathan had two more slabs of venison sizzling in the

46

frying pan. A kettle of beans bubbled in a pot, and the aroma of coffee filled the cabin. When the girl emerged from her room, Nathan pointed to the basin and suggested she wash her hands for supper. The suggestion was met with a look of surprise. The trapper then went to the basin himself, poured water in it, and rewashed his own hands. Somewhat reluctantly she did the same, and they went to the table to eat.

The bread and meat were the same as they had for breakfast, but the beans were new to the girl. So was the spoon by her plate. He quickly used his own spoon so she might get the idea. She watched him eat several spoonfuls, then tried one herself. The sudden grimace on her face made him smile. The girl swallowed what she had in her mouth, but she would not eat another bean.

"You better learn to like beans," Nathan said. "They're a staple around here. Beans most every day."

"Meat and bread are enough for me."

After dinner, Nathan got up and walked to his most prized possessions. After studying the shelf of books, he took one down and brought it back to the table. Tachechana looked with interest as he turned from page to page. Finally, he found the place for which he was looking, and turned the book around so she could see it. On one page was a fine drawing of a horse, which made the girl's face light up. She pointed to the markings on the facing page.

"What are these?" she asked, thinking the marks looked like large black bugs marching across the page.

"Words."

"What do they say?"

"They are white man's words, called English."

"Are there no words in the Sioux tongue?"

"Not written in a book."

"Why?"

"There is no one of the Sioux who could read the words if the books were written."

"When I learn to read will someone make the words in the Sioux tongue for me to read?"

"You will first have to learn English. Then it may be that you will teach others to read, and you will make books in the Sioux language."

The girl thought long on this. "When will we begin?" she asked.

"Tomorrow," said the trapper with a smile. "First we must sleep."

Nathan picked up the dishes and utensils from the table and took them to the dry sink cupboard, washed and dried them, and set them aside for the night. He reached in behind a box in the cupboard and produced a candle. After lighting it he handed it to Tachechana and indicated it was time for her to go to her room.

Nathan was a long time getting to sleep. *How did I ever get myself into this?* he thought. *Can I teach her English, much less to read, and then translate into Sioux?* Though plagued by doubt, he knew this had been one of the most interesting days he had experienced since he took up the life of a trapper.

"Of course not!"

"Then you are ashamed of yourself?"

"No. It's just not the proper thing to do."

"Who makes it not proper?" the girl asked. Her tone was no longer teasing.

"God. It was God who made it not proper," he finally managed to say.

"Is not the white man's God and the Indian's Great Spirit the same?" she asked.

"Well . . . I suppose so."

"Then why didn't the Great Spirit tell the Indians it wasn't proper?" the girl reasoned.

"I . . . don't know."

Nathan quickly got up and took the blue enameled tin dishes to the dry sink, ending the conversation.

On the way to her room, Tachechana noticed that Nathan had smoothed out his bed. As she did the same, the sun shone through her open shutter, lighting up her room and making her feel comfortable. The girl spotted a nail in the wall not far from the little table Nathan had provided. Pensively, she drew the tomahawk from her sash. The only weapon Nathan carried around the cabin was his belt knife, which he used more as a tool than a weapon. She looked at the tomahawk—then at the nail. Slowly she grasped the "hawk" by its head and hung it on the nail by the thong in its handle. She knew she was safe with the trapper.

Tachechana was startled when she heard the cabin door bang shut. She sprang from her bed and raced into the main room of the cabin. Looking through the small window she saw Nathan on his way to the river carrying two pails. She watched until the path took him into the brush and out of sight. Her eyes stayed fastened to that spot until she saw him reappear. This time the pails were full of water. Not wanting to make him feel spied upon, she jumped back from the window.

When Nathan opened the door, the girl was looking at his shelf of books. "Do you still want to know the white man's words?" he asked.

The look on the girl's face, and the sparks that danced in her eyes answered eloquently. "Does the Gray Head still think he can teach me?"

"Only if we get one thing straight right now. This Gray Head business has to stop. The first word you are to learn is 'Nathan.' My name is Nathan Cooper. But Nathan is what you are to call me."

"Yes, Gray Head Nathan," she replied.

"No! Not Gray Head Nathan, just Nathan."

"But we call each of our fathers Gray Head."

Nathan shook his head. "Call me Nathan."

Watching him carefully Tachechana then asked, "Why doesn't Nathan have a wife to cook for him and carry his water?"

"What?"

"All the young men of the Sioux take wives to do things like cook, and carry water, and . . . make his tepee happy. Why doesn't Nathan have such a wife?"

Nathan's eyes clouded. "I had one once. She died."

Knowing her father's grief over the death of her mother, Tachechana decided to let the subject go for now, but she had an intense desire to learn all she could about white women. That knowledge would help her in some way to understand the mother she never knew.

"It's time we started you on your lessons," he said in a quick attempt to change the subject. "Let's begin by taking care of the horses."

They stepped out of the cabin into a beautiful summer day. It reminded Tachechana of those idyllic days when she rode the Arabian toward the western hills and watched the prairie grass flow in the wind like the waves of a green sea. A pang of loneliness for her father shot through her.

"Since you're so interested in horses I guess that's a good place to begin," Nathan said in Sioux. As he walked up to his stallion, he patted him on the nose. "Horse," he said in English. "Horse."

"Horse?" she replied.

"That's right. Horse."

"Horse," she said with an impish grin.

Nathan showed his amazement at how quickly the girl grasped the meanings of the words. It was almost as if she were teasing him by letting him think she did not already know English. He had no way of knowing she was learning English so she could be more like her mother, and perhaps know her better because of it. Even she didn't realize how strong were her feelings about her mother.

All day the lesson went on. Chores were done. Horses were fed and watered, a small garden patch was cultivated, water was carried up from the river, bread was mixed and set to rise, firewood was split and carried, but all the while the lessons continued. Without even realizing it, Tachechana was doing the work of a squaw. She was so intent on learning her lessons that she didn't think about it until Nathan brought it up.

"I thought you said you would never do squaw's work?" he said as she lifted a bucket of water to the dry sink.

She looked at him, then at her hands with a frown. "Does the white woman help with the house chores?" she asked.

"Yes, the whole family works together."

"I will do my part," she said and the frown turned into a smile.

"I'm sure you will," mused Nathan.

Nathan could do nothing without the cool green eyes of the Indian on him. She wanted to know why he did everything, how it worked, and what would happen next. By the time the evening meal was on the table, Nathan felt drained. He had talked more this day than he had for the last six months.

It was not until the simple meal was complete that Tachechana's curiosity was satisfied for the day. She followed Nathan out of the cabin and up the hill behind it.

The evening was perfect. A slight breeze was blowing from the forest, carrying with it the smells of the wild flowers that bloomed there. The sun was just about to sink below the purple hills to the west, and the birds were singing their evening vespers. The few clouds had turned from gold to pink, to salmon, to purple, and night hushed the birds. The cricket and katydid orchestra tuned up for the nightly concert.

Nothing was said as the two sat enjoying this part of the day. Each understood the specialness of this moment to the other, and both respected the other's right to his own thoughts.

An owl hooted and broke their reverie. They looked up and saw the sky spangled with stars against black velvet.

Slowly, without a word, Nathan rose from the boulder upon which he was sitting and turned toward the cabin. Tachechana followed a short distance behind, the first time she had ever walked behind a man.

Once back at the cabin Nathan lit the coal oil lamps and began his nightly ritual of setting things in order for the next day. Every move he made was noted by Tachechana. It made Nathan feel somewhat uncomfortable. Finally he said that it was time to go to sleep.

She nodded and started for her room, but turned just before she got there. She walked back to Nathan and stretched out her right hand toward him. Not knowing what she wanted, he extended his. She grasped his right wrist and gave it a firm tug downward. Nathan understood the move and smiled at her. It was the Indian form of shaking hands as one would do with a friend. He stood and watched as she turned and the worn blanket that was her door closed behind her.

Chapter
6

NATHAN FOUND SLEEP ELUSIVE. The reference to his wife made him twist and turn. Long ago events he had tried to put out of his mind now returned to haunt him. He knew he would never truly understand the things he had done, and that he deserved to be plagued by the memory of them. But for how long?

Whiskey was not the answer to his problem. He had tried that, but it only increased his shame. Hard work only forestalled the inevitable memories. Solitude seemed to be his answer. Here in the lovely lonely wilderness there were no people to remind him of his past shame. Now, an Indian girl was bringing back a tidal wave of memories. As he slept fitfully the pleading look on his wife's face that last time he saw her etched itself in his dreams.

Long before dawn he awoke and lay in his bed for what seemed an eternity waiting for the sunrise and the activity that would occupy his mind. Still he could not drive away the haunting face that condemned him.

He heard the night creatures singing their songs as they did that terrible night so long ago. An occasional coyote interrupted the symphony. Most of all he remembered the sound made by his horse's hooves as he galloped away from his house of horror.

Just when he thought he could stand it no longer, he began to notice that he could see the various objects inside the cabin. Dawn had at last arrived. Quietly he slipped from his bed and out the door. By force of habit he scanned the entire countryside to be sure there were no surprises awaiting him. He hated surprises. Satisfied he was alone, he proceeded down the path to the makeshift outhouse.

When Nathan reentered the cabin he was amused to find Tachechana, her eyes still sleepy, busy at building a fire in the stove.

"Does the daughter of a Great Chief cook food for a white man?" he asked with a grin. She saw he was teasing and tried to look angry.

"She does if that is the only way she will have food for herself," she said.

"Then I will take over the job."

She already had a good fire going, so Nathan began to make some pancakes. Nothing was said as he mixed the ingredients, but he noticed her green eyes watching his every move. How anxious she was to learn everything she could about his way of life. To his surprise, she got the old, blue enameled dishes out and set them on the table along with a fork and spoon for each of them. She even set out two coffee cups.

Nathan took that cue and filled the cups with coffee. It tickled him to see her grasp the cup in both hands and warm her fingers the way he always did.

As the last of the batter was browning to perfection in

the frying pan, Nathan brought the stack of pancakes to the table. He crossed back to the dry sink and reached under it for a very special half gallon crockery jug. The girl watched. He took three pancakes off the stack and put them on his plate. Carefully he poured a good quantity of the syrup from the crock onto the pancakes and passed the jug over to the girl. With her finger she tasted the amber fluid.

Nathan almost burst into laughter at the look of pure joy on her face.

"What is this?" she asked in careful English.

"Maple syrup."

"Good!" she lapsed back into her native tongue. "Where do you get it?"

"From trees."

She looked straight into his eyes for several seconds before she was sure he was serious. Then she attacked the food as if she hadn't eaten for days.

After finishing his breakfast, Nathan emptied the last of the water from the buckets to wash the dishes. Without a word or a glance in his direction, she took the two buckets and headed for the river. As the door banged behind her the trapper almost broke out laughing at the sight of the girl who wouldn't do squaw's work.

It took her much longer to get the water than it should have, but Nathan wasn't concerned. Nor was he about to go near the river while she was there.

He finished the dishes and straightened his blankets. Just as he was about to care for the horses, she arrived back at the cabin. Her hair was wet and there were wet spots on her deerskin breeches and shirt.

Together they walked out to the horse shed and turned

61

the horses loose to graze on the fresh grass on the southeast side of the building. At night the animals were confined to the shed and a smaller corral between the shed and the cabin. There was one more pasture on the west side. It needed no fence as the horses were confined by a rock box canyon on three sides and the shed, corral, and cabin on the fourth. Nathan always saved that pasture for emergency use. The only way anyone could approach the cabin was from the front. Nathan did not like surprises.

Nathan took this opportunity to study the Arabian mare, a truly magnificent animal. She was so dark a brown she appeared black. The white blaze on her face hung down over one side of her nose. Her eyes, bright and alert, followed Tachechana's every movement.

All Indians loved their horses, but this horse obviously loved in return. The only white spot other than on her nose was on the hind foot, but not high enough to be called a stocking. From her proud head to her flowing tail she was a marvelous specimen. Nathan knew the braves of Tachechana's village would not let such a prize get away.

He turned to the girl and resumed the lessons: "What is this?" he asked as he picked up his saddle and sat it on the fence.

"Saddle," she said.

"Good."

He took a tin from the shelf in the horse shed and began to rub the paste it contained into the shiny brown leather. All the while he worked on the saddle, he kept asking, "What is this?"

"Stone."

"What is this?"

"Fence."

"What is this?"

"Horse!" She never forgot horse.

Then it was her turn to ask, "What is this?" and Nathan added more words to her English vocabulary. Some of the English words would make her giggle. Others piqued her interest and she would ask, "Why?"

"Because it is," was Nathan's answer most of the time.

As the shadows began to lengthen, Nathan told the girl to get her horse ready for a ride. Quickly he saddled Rowdy, then went into the cabin. From the rafters above his bed he produced a fine split bamboo fishing rod. After catching a few grasshoppers, much to Tachechana's amusement, they mounted up and headed for a small feeder stream about one mile up the river from the cabin.

Nathan carefully threaded one of the grasshoppers onto a fine wire hook and slowly made his way to a deep hole. He plopped the grasshopper down in the still water behind an old log. It made fewer than five kicks when a shadow slowly rose from the deepest part of the pool. It sucked the grasshopper, hook and all, into its mouth. He twitched the rod to set the hook and the fight was on.

After a moment or two of thrashing on the end of the line, the plump trout jumped once, twice, and lay on the top of the pool, thrashing its head from side to side. Nathan slid it onto the bank and thrust one prong of a forked stick through its gills and out its mouth. He held it up for Tachechana to see. The girl was unimpressed.

She explained to Nathan how her people made traps by driving stakes into the streambed forming a funnel shaped maze. The fish could swim in with ease, but could not find

63

their way out. Then the natives would either spear the fish or simply catch them in their hands.

"That's no sport," he told her. "Here, you try it."

He threaded another grasshopper on the hook and handed the rod to the girl. Immediately she hung the bug up in a small tree on the far side of the stream.

Nathan waded across and retrieved it. He knew he scared all the trout from that hole, so they moved upstream. This time she got the grasshopper to the water where it was instantly inhaled by a large trout.

"Look!" she shrieked as the beautiful trout leaped clear of the water and cartwheeled in midair. When she landed the fish, the look of pride and happiness on her face delighted Nathan.

"Bigger than yours," she said with a grin.

"Yep," was all the answer she got. He knew how she felt, and he suspected she would never trap trout again, unless it was an emergency. They mounted their horses and headed back to the cabin.

Perhaps it was the excitement at the pool, or maybe they were a little careless, but neither Nathan nor Tachechana realized that other eyes had seen their activity at the stream. High on the hill on the opposite side of the stream sat birdlike Eagle Feather. He was not aware anyone was in the area until he heard the excited cry of Tachechana below him.

Eagle Feather, who was the first to ask for Tachechana to be his wife, had been searching for over a week in the hills for her. Now, as he sat resting, she had almost come to him. But he was deeply concerned that she was in the company of the trapper. He acknowledged to himself that his task of persuading her to return to the village as his wife as required by her father would now be more difficult. But he knew his job would not be an easy one when he began.

He watched them as they rode down the stream to the river and turned south. There was no need to follow them now, for they were making no effort to conceal their tracks. He could track them later when there would be no danger of being seen.

Back at the cabin, while Nathan cleaned the fish, Tachechana built a small fire outside. He was surprised when the girl took the fish from him. She impaled them on a green stick and held the body cavity open with other smaller green sticks. While the fire burned down to hot glowing coals, she gave the trapper a lesson in Indian cookery.

Accepting his secondary role, the trapper went inside, heated the coffee and set the table.

Within moments the girl entered with two of the most succulent golden brown trout that Nathan had ever seen. He added a touch of salt to the fish, tasted one, and thought he had died and gone to heaven.

"You are a very good cook," he told her.

"Many times I have seen my father, Great Bear, cook fish this way."

"Your father is a Great Chief."

"How do you know of my father?"

"Not far from where you caught the fish today, I met your father. It was almost a year ago. I was fishing and did not know he was there. A large fish had taken my bait and I was bringing it to the bank. There was a large rattlesnake resting on a stone. I didn't see it, but just before I would have stepped on it, I heard the twang of a bow. Your father's arrow killed the snake and I lost the fish. Since then we have seen each other several times on the trail. He is a good man."

Something began to gnaw at the pit of Nathan's stomach. Had he been careless at the stream? If Great Bear could get so close to him while fishing, couldn't some other Indian have done the same today? Perhaps one that might not be as friendly as the Chief? Nathan had not been his usual cautious self in the excitement of teaching his new friend the art of trout fishing.

When he finished eating, he walked to the door of the cabin and studied each tree, bush, and rock. The night, however, was settling in and he could not make out the dark form of an Indian partly obscured by the foliage.

"I'll have to be more careful from now on," he muttered to himself.

Back inside the cabin he asked Tachechana when she had lost her tomahawk.

"It is not lost," she replied. "It's hanging on a peg in the trap room."

"Why didn't you carry it at all today?"

"You are a friend of my father and me. I did not need it."

"Yes, I am your friend, but you might have enemies out there."

She looked startled. "You had only your knife," she replied. "Don't you fear the Sioux and Arapaho?"

"I don't think the Sioux or Arapaho know where we are, but we must not be careless." He got up and walked to the wall where his tomahawk hung. He took it from the wall and stuck its ash handle in his belt. Stepping back to the table he poured himself another cup of coffee and sat with both hands wrapped around the cup. Tachechana also wrapped her fingers around her cup.

Out in the darkness Eagle Feather sat contemplating his next move. Now that he had found Tachechana, how was he going to persuade her to return to the village as his wife? Was she already the wife of the trapper? *No,* he thought. *That could not be true.* But how could he talk to her if the trapper was always there?

When deep darkness finally came, he carefully picked his way back to where he had tethered his horse. He would make his camp for the night in the hidden grove above the trout stream where he had first seen them. He would come back tomorrow and search for a way to talk to the girl he wished would be his wife.

Once back at his hiding place Eagle Feather recalled Great Bear's warning that no harm was to come to his daughter. Eagle Feather wanted no harm to come to her either. While it would be great to own her horse, the real reason he was on this trip was to win the girl for his wife.

But, thought Eagle Feather, *Great Bear said nothing about the trapper. And he, too, has a fine horse. A horse almost as fast as The Fox. If the white man must be killed to get the girl, he will be killed.*

After a cold meal of venison jerky and a long drink of water, Eagle Feather wrapped himself in his blanket and went to sleep.

That evening Nathan let Tachechana turn through the

pages of several of his books. She was obsessed with learning to read. Of course she could not understand one word, but she stopped at every illustration and named every object she could in English. When she reached for the large black volume on the end of the shelf Nathan told her it was time to go to bed. Obediently she replaced the books in their proper order on the shelf and retreated to her room.

As the girl crawled into her bed, she thought of the new words she had learned that day. . . . And she thought of the big fish she caught the white man's way. . . . And she thought of her father. She wondered why he had not told her that he, too, had saved the white man's life. She wondered *why* he had saved the white man's life. She wondered why she had saved the white man's life.

On the other side of the trap room door Nathan did some wondering too. He wondered why he let the girl stay with him. . . . And why he didn't want her to handle his dusty Bible. . . . And why he had been so careless today. . . . And if there were Indian eyes watching his cabin at that very moment. He wondered why he had been such a coward. . . . Would he ever be able to shed the memory of his wife's anguished face?

Chapter
7

BOTH NATHAN AND TACHECHANA AWOKE at the same time. It was still dark, but they had both gotten up and met at the front door. Neither of them said a word. The Fox nickered. Rowdy pawed the ground.

"Storm coming," said Nathan, and he walked outside to secure the horses in the shed. The girl was at his side. She knew her horse would give the trapper a bad time if she were not there. Together they led the horses into the shelter and slid the handcrafted bolt into place.

"No need for them to be wet and cold," said Nathan.

Tachechana thought that a bit strange. The Indians never had shelter for their horses. Many times she had watched the wild horses seemingly enjoy a good summer rain. *Is not rain as natural for horses as sunshine?* she thought. But if the trapper said to take the horses into the cabin, she would have done it to please him. *Why is it so important to me that I please him?* she wondered.

Back inside the cabin neither of them seemed ready to go back to sleep. Nathan lit the coal oil lamp and they both sat at the table. Several moments went by with neither of them saying a word. Yet there was no awkwardness between them.

"Is the shutter on your window closed?" asked Nathan.

"No," said Tachechana as she got up to close it.

"No sense letting your bed get wet."

When she came back into the main room of the cabin Nathan asked if she wanted something to eat. She declined, but Nathan went to his cupboard and got two black pieces of jerky. He took a bite of one and handed the other to Tachechana. The girl took it and ate it. It was a bit more salty than the jerky made by her people, but good considering it was made by a white man.

She mentally noted that Nathan was skilled at doing most things that were handled by squaws in her village, yet she perceived him as strong and gentle. That was a strange combination for a man. Yet she saw some of this gentleness in her father. Could it be because of his association with white people? Her thoughts went to her mother. Did women really have that much control over men?

Nathan went to the water bucket and took a long drink from the ladle. The salt from the jerky had made Tachechana thirsty, too. She followed his lead. One of the main benefits of eating jerky was that it made you thirsty. The water you drank swelled the dried meat in your stomach and gave you a nice full feeling even though you only ate a little.

When Tachechana turned from the water bucket, Nathan was sitting on his bed. Thinking he was tired she retreated to her own room and crawled into bed. Nathan blew out the lamp and each went back to sleep.

Shortly before daybreak thunder rumbled through the hills like a giant with indigestion. The tempo of the storm increased with crescendo after crescendo, punctuated with cymbal crashes of lightning. The trees danced to the melody of the wind, swaying gently at first, then violently as the song became a screaming moan. The trees seemed to be clapping their hands until, as if by exhaustion, one would crash to the earth. The others continued the dance until the wind finished its song and the drumbeat of the rain diminished to a gentle falling mist.

Finally the sun broke out of its confinement in the clouds and the trees rested in its warmth. The earth lapped up the puddles. Before darkness came it was almost impossible to tell there had been a storm.

Throughout the day the two occupants of the cabin stayed indoors. Nathan tore some pages from the tablet he sometimes used as a diary and dug through his belongings until he found the stub of a pencil. Carefully he drew the letters of the alphabet while Tachechana watched.

"A," he said as he drew that letter.

"What is 'A'?" she asked.

"A letter."

"What is a letter?"

"Letters are what words are made of," Nathan said.

"B," he continued.

"Is 'B' a letter, too?"

"Yes."

"Why?"

"Because it is! There are this many letters you must learn," he said as he made twenty-six straight scratch marks on the paper.

"Are they letters, too?"

"No, they are just marks," he said with a sigh.

They moved on through the alphabet with Nathan

drawing the letter, saying it, and Tachechana repeating it until he got to "I."

"I thought you said those marks were not letters," she said, pointing to the twenty-six scratch marks.

"They're not."

"What is this?" she said, pointing to the I.

"I," he said.

"Why is it 'i' here, and not there? They look the same."

"All right. If you want to call the scratch marks 'I' you may."

"May I call 'A,' 'I'?"

"No."

"Why?"

"Because 'A' is 'A' and 'I' is 'I.' "

"Oh," she said, but she didn't understand why she could call scratch marks "I" but not "A."

Nathan stopped for a moment and thought. This time he drew a capital A and a small A. "These are 'A,' " he said.

"Both of them?"

"Yes."

"How can two different letters have the same name?"

Nathan buried his face in his hands. He went to the book shelf and took down one of the books. He turned to two pictures of women. One was tall and slender, the other short and stocky. "What is this?" he asked, pointing to the tall one.

"Woman."

"And what is this?" he said pointing to the short one.

"Woman!" she said with a smile. "One big, the other little."

"It's the same with letters. All of them can be 'Tall,' or 'Small.' "

The relief on Nathan's face made Tachechana giggle.

He wrote, or rather drew, the first five letters on the top line of another piece of paper. When Tachechana could name them all, he gave her the pencil and told her to copy them on the paper.

She was eager to try. Nathan got up to get a drink.

"Nathan."

"What?"

"This stick won't make letters."

Apprehension was all over her face when he turned to see what the problem was. She had broken the point by pressing too hard. She thought she had ruined it, and now would never be able to learn to read.

Nathan took out his knife and whittled a new point on the pencil. When he gave it back to her, he showed her how to hold it and told her not to press so hard. She was very interested in how easily the point was restored.

"It's too bad we can't do that when a horse breaks its leg," she said, as she went back to her paper.

Eagle Feather lay on a buffalo skin in the wet brush about two hundred yards from the door of Nathan's cabin. Rather he lay on part of it and the other part was folded over on top of him.

He wanted desperately to talk to Tachechana, but didn't have any idea how he might accomplish it. Perhaps she would come out alone and he might signal her. He had no way of knowing how busily she was working on the white man's language inside the cabin.

If the white man is a friend of Tachechana, he will not permit me to talk with her, he thought. *He must die, but if I kill him, she will not listen to me.* His mind was racing for an idea of how he might kill the man and not have Tachechana know about it.

Perhaps I can make the trapper have an accident. When he goes to the river, I could hold him under and she would think he drowned. Or, if he catches fish again I can push stones down the mountain on him. All the time he plotted Nathan's death, he stared at the seemingly lifeless cabin. The only sign of activity all morning was the two grazing horses.

As the afternoon grew to a close, he noticed smoke start its lazy swirl out of the chimney and up the rock walls behind the cabin. Eagle Feather knew they were preparing the evening meal and felt himself getting hungry.

The door of the cabin opened and Eagle Feather flattened himself as low as he could in the brush. He could make out the form of Nathan in the doorway. The trapper was just standing there surveying the territory before committing himself to step into the open. Finally satisfied, he stepped out and down the trail to the river. He was carrying two buckets.

Eagle Feather followed him with his eyes, but did not dare to move lest the girl still be watching from the cabin. When Nathan disappeared from view, he watched the spot until he returned carrying the water. Eagle Feather knew now that Tachechana was not the old man's squaw or she would be carrying the water. That made him feel much better about trying to win her heart.

When Nathan reentered the cabin Eagle Feather felt he had seen enough for one day and slowly slipped back into the brush and to his horse. He needed time now to plan how he was to get rid of the trapper.

Back inside the cabin Tachechana had finished her paper of Aa, Bb, Cc, Dd, and Ee. Proudly she held it up for Nathan to see. He was surprised, no, amazed at how quickly she had learned to make her fingers do what her eyes had seen. Beneath his hand drawn letters she had filled the page with exact duplicates of them. But what surprised him most of all was the small sketch she made in the bottom corner of the paper. Almost as a signature on the bottom was the drawing of the head and neck of a horse, its mane blowing in the wind.

"What is that on the bottom?" he asked.

Tachechana appeared embarrassed. "It is a picture of The Fox," she said, half apologetically.

"It is a very good picture."

Her green eyes sparkled as she received the praise of her teacher. He was pleased with her marks.

Tachechana rushed through her meal of venison and corn meal muffins that Nathan had baked. The trapper noticed her haste and sensed her eagerness to return to her work.

"While I wash the dishes you can do another page of letters," he said, then smiled when he saw her eager response. He intended to place a row of letters on the top of the page for her, but by the time he had cleared the table, she had already started to write the letters from memory. Her keen mind always seemed to be a step or two ahead of him.

What am I going to teach you after you know more than I do? he thought to himself. *The way you are going it might be next week. .*

When she finished that page of letters, she again made a

75

sketch of a horse's head and neck on the bottom. She held it up in front of her at arm's length and smiled. Nathan smiled, too. He took the paper from her and turned it over.

"F," he said and wrote Ff.

"F," she replied.

"Gg, Hh, Ii, Jj," he wrote and named them. Each time she replied. She almost snatched the pencil out of his hand when she saw that it was her turn to write.

"Be careful! You must do it neatly or other people will not know what you are trying to say."

She slowed down and began drawing each letter, repeating its name as she drew it.

While she worked on the second five letters he had given her, Nathan took down one of his books from the shelf. He began reading it where it fell open.

"Are you reading the marks?" Tachechana asked.

"Yes."

"What do they say?"

"It is a poem about some Indians who live far to the east."

"A white man has written about Indians?"

"Yes."

"What does it say?"

Nathan began reading, filling in with the Sioux language as best he could.

> Listen to the words of wisdom,
> Listen to the words of warning,
> From the lips of the Great Spirit,
> From the Master of Life who made you!
> "I have given you lands to hunt in,
> I have given you streams to fish in,
> I have given you bear and bison,

I have given you roe and reindeer,
I have given you brant and beaver,
Filled the marshes full of wild fowl,
Filled the rivers full of fishes;
Why then are you not content?
Why then will you hunt each other?
I am weary of your quarrels,
Weary of your wars and bloodshed,
Weary of your prayers for vengeance,
Of your wranglings and dissensions;
All your strength is in your union,
All your danger is in discord;
Therefore be at peace henceforward
And as brothers live together. . . .

"Bathe now in the stream before you,
Wash the warpaint from your faces,
Wash the bloodstains from your fingers,
Bury your war-clubs and your weapons,
Break the redstone from this quarry,
Mold and make it into Peace Pipes,
Take the reeds that grow beside you,
Deck them with your brightest feathers,
Smoke the calumet together,
And as brothers live henceforward!"

Nathan looked up from the book to get the girl's reaction. Her eyes were filled with wonder, her mouth half open. "Go on, read more," she whispered.

Then upon the ground the warriors
Threw their cloaks and shirts of deerskin,
Threw their weapons and their war-gear,
Leaped into the rushing river,
Washed the warpaint from their faces.
Clear above them flowed the water,

Clear and limpid from the footprints
Of the Master of Life descending;
Dark below them flowed the water,
Soiled and stained with streaks of crimson,
As if blood were mingled with it!
From the river came the warriors,
Clean and washed from all their warpaint;
On the banks their clubs they buried,
Buried all their warlike weapons.
Gitche Manito, the mighty,
The Great Spirit, the creator,
Smiled upon his helpless children!

Tachechana could not understand all the words Nathan read in English. Some of them he explained in Sioux as he read. But she understood enough to get the sense of the poem.

"Does the Great Spirit want the Sioux to bury their weapons?" she asked.

"It would be fine if all men buried their weapons and lived at peace."

"Is that why you did not kill all of us on the prairie the other day?"

"No . . . that is . . . I don't know."

"Has the Great Spirit ever spoken to you, Nathan?"

"Yes, but not with his voice."

"What do you mean?"

"He has given us a Book."

"Do you have that Book?"

"Yes."

"Which one is it? You must read it often!"

"It's the black one on the end, and I hardly ever read it."

"Why?"

"You had better go back to writing your letters."

Tachechana looked at him in surprise, dropped the subject and went back to her studies.

Nathan, however, could not think of anything but the hard questions she had put to him. He knew why he didn't read his Bible. It told the truth about himself. And it was desperately hard for him to reconcile the fact that at one time he thought he might become a preacher of that Bible and its story.

When Tachechana finished her page and retired to her room, Nathan breathed a sigh of relief. He looked over to the bookshelf at his Bible. *Maybe I should read it once in a while,* he thought. He took the volume of Longfellow he had been reading and returned it to its place on the shelf. He almost had his hand on the Bible, to take it down, to read, when his hand began to shake. It was not fear. Or was it? Was he afraid to face up to what the Bible said about him?

He turned on his heel and stomped rather than walked back to the table. Sitting there with his face in his hands, he rehearsed again the events of the night he left his wife at the mercy of the two intruders. Why had he feared so for his life? Now he knew the truth of the statement, "Brave men die once, cowards die every day."

He didn't even notice when the lamp flickered out for want of oil. He sat there in the darkness seeking relief for his stricken conscience as the tears came. "Why? . . . Why?"

Tachechana thought she had done something wrong when she asked about the black Book. On the way to her room she looked at the Book on the end of the shelf, but didn't dare touch it. It was obviously a sacred Book and only to be handled by the wise ones. Still she couldn't figure out why Nathan didn't read the words from the Great Spirit whom he called God.

Later she woke up to the sobbing of the trapper. She was puzzled. Why would so strong a man as Nathan cry? She wanted to go out and comfort him, but she felt it might shame him for someone to see him cry. She lay in her bed knowing she had nothing to say that would comfort him. All she could do was hurt with him.

Chapter
8

NATHAN WOKE UP RED-EYED and grumpy. He hardly spoke as Tachechana came from her room. Breakfast was eaten in almost total silence. No mention was made by either of them about the conversation and events of the previous night.

When the meal was over Tachechana left to fill the buckets and invigorate her body in the cold water of the river. Nathan was glad to be alone. The talk of God and the Bible had stirred up many memories, most of which convicted him. Several times while washing the dishes and cleaning up the cabin, his eyes wandered to the Book in its place on the shelf. "This is stupid!" he said aloud and stomped out the door. Picking up his ax, he began to split wood for the stove.

Tachechana heard the crack of his ax on wood all the way across the river where she had been swimming. She swam back, got into her shirt and breeches, gathered up the water buckets and headed back to the cabin. After putting the water buckets on the dry sink, she went out and began stacking the wood in front of the cabin where the overhanging roof would keep it dry.

Most of the morning Nathan continued his wood chopping without saying a word. He would chop, she would stack. When the trapper laid down his ax for a rest, she picked it up. As he reached for it, she would not let it go.

"What have I done to make you angry?" she asked.

"Nothing." He tugged on the ax handle, but she held it tight. He had to look into her eyes. There he saw the same pleading look he saw in the eyes of his wife some twenty years ago.

"Why are you angry with me?"

"I am not angry with you. I am angry with myself."

"At yourself?"

"Yes! Why don't you leave me alone!"

The girl's face was stricken. She released her grip on the ax and went into the cabin. Nathan resumed his chopping.

A short time later Tachechana appeared in the doorway carrying all of her belongings and headed toward the horse shed.

Nathan looked up from his chopping with surprise. "What are you doing?" he asked.

"I am leaving you alone," she said.

"I didn't mean you had to leave, just let me be by myself."

"How can I let you be by yourself, if I stay?"

Nathan realized how badly he had hurt the girl's feelings. "I am not angry with you," he repeated. "It is just that I am feeling sorry for myself."

"Why do you feel so sorry?"

"If you knew, you would hate me and never want to see me again."

"You have been a friend," the girl said. "When an Indian has a friend, that friend is hers in spite of everything. Am I a friend to you?"

"Yes," he admitted. His shoulders sagged and his eyes dropped to the ground. "But I have been a terrible man in the past."

"You are a good man now."

"Thank you, but that's not true. I am still an evil man."

"You have been good to me, and your horse. You could have killed me and the braves the other day, but you didn't. How can you say you are evil?"

The ax slipped through Nathan's fingers. He walked to the small rail fence that stretched from the cabin to the horse shed. With his forearms on the top rail and one foot on the bottom rail, he looked at the stone walls that protected them from the west. For a long time he stared and said nothing. The girl stood behind him, trying to help him, but not knowing how.

"Why did a brave man like you cry last night?" she asked.

"I cried because I am not a brave man. I cried because I am a coward!"

"No white man who is a coward would choose to live in the land of the Sioux. You have faced death many times."

Nathan could hold it back no longer. "Long ago, when I was a young man," he began, "I married a fine woman. We were very happy together. Then one night two men rode up to our home. They burst in and demanded to be fed. Thinking they would leave after they were filled, I asked my wife to feed them. As they ate, it came out that they had escaped from prison.

"After the men had eaten, they made advances toward

my wife, remarking how long it had been since they had been with a woman. I tried to deter them, but one of the escaped prisoners pulled out a gun and threatened to kill me if I didn't do exactly as they said. This man held the gun on me while the other took my wife into the bedroom.

"I had to sit there, staring into the cruel eyes of the criminal, listening to the cries and sobs of my loved one. When the men exchanged places, my agony overwhelmed me. I became sick at my stomach, then bolted out the front door. For some reason I was not shot. Perhaps the gun wasn't loaded. Outside, I jumped on my horse and galloped into the night for help. It took me an hour to find the sheriff. When we returned, the escaped prisoners were gone and my wife was dead.

"I left town shortly thereafter and have been running ever since. I cannot get away from my shame for not fighting for the life and honor of the woman I loved."

With the story out, Nathan fell again into his deep silence. Tachechana tried to share in his sorrow. She reached out and laid her hand on his shoulder tenderly. When he turned and saw compassion in her eyes rather than scorn, he was surprised.

"Many times my people have been beaten in a battle, but that doesn't make them cowards," she said. "They go back and fight again. A true warrior is not the one who always wins, but one who tries to win after he has been beaten. You may have lost one battle, but you have shown bravery by coming to live in the land of the Sioux and Arapaho."

"But I live with fear each day. I was frightened the day you brought my horse back to me. I fear death right now. How can anyone think me anything but a coward?"

"Do you fear me?"

"No."

"Do you fear the horses?"

"No."

"Did you fear the storm yesterday?"

"No."

"There are many things you do not fear. Why do you call yourself a coward?"

"Because I left my wife at the mercy of those men and they killed her."

"When my people have been defeated, they ask the Great Spirit why, and ask to be given another chance. Is this the way of the white man and his God?"

For a long time Nathan didn't say anything. Finally he said, "It is more than just being defeated. I have done an evil thing. God doesn't want anything to do with the likes of me."

"Then the white man's God is not the Great Spirit of the Indian. The Giver of Life is always concerned about his children. What you read last night from the book shows that."

Nathan shook his head. "No," he said. "Both are the same. I wish I could believe there is hope for me."

"Did you not say the black Book on the end of the shelf was your God's words?"

"Yes."

"Then the answer is there. You must read it."

Her logic was so overwhelmingly simple that Nathan considered the possibility that he was the heathen and she the Christian. "I will read it tonight," he said.

Tachechana spent the rest of the day watching him cut

wood and then stacking it in front of the cabin. When that space was filled, she stacked it in front of the horse shed.

It was almost evening before Nathan had erased the self-hate from his system. He marveled at how hard the girl had worked without a word of complaint.

"Let's fix something to eat," he said.

Together they walked along the river to a small marsh. Nathan began tugging at the cattails along the shore. Up came large tuberous roots that he cut away from the stems and tossed on shore. When he had about three or four pounds of them he picked them up and he and the girl headed back to the cabin.

"Fill that large pot with water and put it on the stove," he told Tachechana. He began to peel the skinlike membrane from the roots and cut the white centers into cubes. The skins were thrown away and the white cubes put into the large pot. While they were boiling, he made a fresh pot of coffee and began to fry some venison steaks.

When the steaks were done, he took them from the pan and poured some of the water from the cattail roots into the frying pan. Tachechana jumped as the pan hissed loudly when the water was poured into it and a cloud of steam hovered over and around the stove. Into the mixture of meat juices and cattail water Nathan stirred a small amount of flour and water. The liquid thickened into a rich gravy.

He put two big scoops of the cubes and a venison steak in each of the blue enameled bowls and then nearly filled the bowls with the gravy. Pieces of bread were added and they both sat down to eat.

Nathan hesitated before he began to eat; a strange look came to his face.

"What is wrong?" she asked.

"Nothing. I just thought . . . maybe . . . we should thank God—the Great Spirit—for the food He has given us."

"How?"

"We call it prayer," he said. "We close our eyes and tell God we are grateful for what He has given us."

She closed her eyes.

"Lord," Nathan began, "we don't deserve any favors from you, but we thank you for giving us this food. Bless us with it, and . . . make us into the kind of people you would have us to be. Amen."

Nathan looked up, but the girl still had her eyes closed. "When I say 'Amen' it means I am finished," he said. She looked up with a radiant smile.

"Is that all there is to talking to God?"

"Yes," Nathan replied, noticing that she used only the white man's name for the Deity. *Am I doing her a wrong by forcing my ways on her?* he thought.

As they ate, Tachechana mentioned how good the cattails and gravy were. He told her that cattails were wilderness potatoes. "Later in the summer, we will gather many of them to use after the snows come."

After supper he got out a sheet of paper and the pencil stub. "See if you can make all the letters I showed you last night," he said.

When the dishes were washed, he looked to see how many letters she had forgotten. To his amazement both sides of the paper were covered with all the letters he had shown her. In the lower right-hand corner of each side of the paper was the usual head and flying mane of a horse . . . her horse.

He tore another page from the tablet. "Kk, Ll, Mm, Nn, Oo," he said. She giggled, pointing to the small L and said "I." He, too, chuckled, remembering his frustration of the previous night. She repeated the names of these letters and he gave her the pencil. He walked to the bookshelf and took down Longfellow again.

"Not that one," the girl said.

"Why?"

"The black one on the end."

Nathan stared at her. She was smiling a pleading sort of smile and he returned Longfellow to its place and took down the dusty, old Bible. His hands shook as he held it and he didn't know where to begin.

The Bible fell open to Psalm 47. Nathan read the first verse to himself.

"O clap your hands, all ye people; shout unto God with the voice of triumph. . . ." No, that's not what he needed. He looked at Psalm 48.

"Great is the Lord, and greatly to be praised in the city of our God. . . ." Not that one either. Psalm 49 started, "Hear this, all ye people; give ear, all ye inhabitants of the world. . . ."

There must be something in here for me, he thought as he went on to Psalm 50.

"The mighty God, even the Lord, hath spoken. . . ." His eyes slipped down to Psalm 51.

"Have mercy upon me, O God, according to thy loving-kindness!" What he needed suddenly was unfolding before his eyes. "According unto the multitude of thy tender mercies blot out my transgressions. Wash me thoroughly from mine iniquity, and cleanse me from my sin."

Nathan's heart pounded. Was this the message God had for him? He carefully read on. "For I acknowledge my transgressions: and my sin is ever before me. Against thee, thee only, have I sinned, and done this evil in thy sight."

Nathan was reading the words of Scripture, but it was becoming the prayer of his heart.

"Purge me with hyssop, and I shall be clean: wash me, and I shall be whiter than snow. Make me to hear joy and gladness; that the bones which thou hast broken may rejoice.

"Hide thy face from my sins, and blot out all mine iniquities. Create in me a clean heart, O God; and renew a right spirit within me." He was beginning to breathe faster as he read. It was as if he were talking to the Almighty, Himself.

"Restore unto me the joy of thy salvation; and uphold me with thy free spirit. Then will I teach transgressors thy ways; and sinners shall be converted unto thee. Deliver me from blood-guiltiness, O God, thou God of my salvation. . . . The sacrifices of God are a broken spirit: a broken and a contrite heart, O God, thou wilt not despise."

Nathan read the passage a second time, then a third. He was so engrossed he didn't even know Tachechana was there, much less that she had finished the paper and was now watching his every move. Tears began to fill his eyes.

Nathan finally closed the Book and walked outside. The stars were blazing their glory and a sliver of the new moon hung in the southeastern sky.

"God, if you can still care about me as the Bible says, please forgive me. I know I have no right to ask, but I'm sorry for my past life. I sinned over and over again."

There, under the canopy of God's vastness, Nathan poured out his heart to his Creator.

Relief came to him like a fresh breeze from the mountains. For the first time in almost twenty years Nathan felt at peace with himself and his God. He turned and went into the cabin.

Both sides of Tachechana's paper were covered with new letters and in the lower right corner of each page was the usual horse head. Along the edge of the paper was a tangled vine of flowers. These she had absent-mindedly sketched while waiting for Nathan's return.

They looked into each other's eyes. Tachechana saw the anguish of the last twenty-four hours was gone. Nathan was refreshed. He smiled. That delighted her and she returned his smile.

"You are happy now?" she asked.

"Yes, very happy."

"Did God talk with you?"

"Yes," Nathan said, "but not the way we talk."

"How did you talk then?"

"I read in the Bible, His Book, that He still loves me, in spite of the bad things that I have done."

She heard that word again and her mind latched onto it. "What is love?"

Nathan was taken aback by the question. "Everyone knows what love is," he said.

"I don't know what it is. My father, the Chief, told me to find out so that I may teach my people."

"Well, love is . . . it's when you like someone or something very much."

"Like The Fox?" she interrupted. "I like The Fox more than anything."

"Yes, I believe you do love your horse, but with God it is more than that."

"No one can like anything more than I like my horse."

"But it's different with God and people."

"Do you not love Rowdy?"

"Yes, I suppose I do. But love between people is greater than when we love an animal or thing, and with God it is even greater."

"People love each other?"

"Yes. The way you feel towards your father is more of what I am saying."

"And my mother?"

"You probably don't remember her."

"But my father has told me about her. She was a fine woman."

"I'm sure she was."

Tachechana sat quietly for several moments.

"Nathan, do you love me?"

"I, ah, that is, I, ah, think you are a very nice person."

"But do you love me?"

"I like you very much."

"That is what you said love was."

"Love has more than just that for a meaning. If liking you very much is the way you mean it, I suppose I do."

"Oh."

The silence was suddenly very awkward. "Let me see your paper," he said.

She handed it to him, wanting to talk more about love, but realizing the subject was difficult for him.

"Why did you make flowers on the sides of the paper?"

"I did it while I was waiting for you to come back."

"Why flowers and not horses?"

"I like flowers, too." She felt almost ashamed of liking flowers. Warriors liked horses and tomahawks, not flowers.

"I like flowers, too," he said and handed the paper back to her. "If you continue to learn your letters this fast you will soon be reading."

The girl beamed.

"Now we must go to bed. There is much work to do tomorrow."

Tachechana retired to her little room with its open window. She looked up into the glittering stars and wondered.

"Great Spirit, do you love me? Does anyone really love me? Teach me what love is."

She blew out her candle and went to sleep.

Eagle Feather walked back to his horse and rode back to camp. He couldn't make any sense of what he saw all day, but he knew he would soon have to talk with Tachechana, regardless of what that cost.

Chapter
9

ALL NIGHT EAGLE FEATHER SCHEMED over how he might rid himself of Nathan. One plan after another focused in his mind, only to be rejected. It seemed that however he planned to kill Nathan, Tachechana was sure to find him responsible. That would put an end to his chance to marry her.

One plan just might work. While looking for Tachechana he had found a small group of Arapaho camping near a stream. If they were still there, he might be able to catch one alone and kill him. He would then take an Arapaho arrow and shoot Nathan with it. Tachechana would know it was an Arapaho arrow and think one of them shot Nathan. He could then show her the Arapaho scalp, and persuade her to return to the village as his wife.

Early in the morning he mounted his horse and headed west. The Arapaho camp had moved since he saw it last, but he had no trouble sorting out their tracks and followed them. They were heading west, deeper into Arapaho territory. He would have to be extremely cautious this far into the enemy's land.

Shortly after noon Eagle Feather smelled smoke. The

Arapaho were camped just ahead. He secured his horse in the densest grove of trees he could find, and taking advantage of every bit of cover, he sneaked to a place where he could see into every part of the small camp.

To his happy surprise the camp was empty except for three squaws. They had just started to build the fire. Eagle Feather knew the men must have just left to hunt for their evening meal. Beside one of the fires was a quiver full of Arapaho arrows. All he had to do was take them.

He almost ran back to his horse and mounted. Slowly he walked his horse, under cover of the brush, back to the camp. When he was just about there, he let out a fierce war cry and dashed in among the three squaws. At this cry they scrambled for the brush, and he rode in and grabbed the arrows. Then with another war whoop he spun his horse and headed back to his own camp.

After he put several miles between himself and the Arapaho camp, he covered his trail by riding on rocks or in streams. He knew the Arapaho would not be able to track him all the way to his campsite pitched on the stream where Nathan and Tachechana fished.

Now he must wait for his chance to get Nathan alone and kill him. He knew he could outwait even the most nervous of game, and Nathan would be no different. The trapper would make a fatal mistake.

The next morning after breakfast Nathan took down his Bible and told Tachechana that he was going to read to her from it. The girl was excited to think that at last she would hear the words of the white man's God.

Nathan thought a moment and turned to the Book of

Psalms. "Move your stool here, next to me, so you can see where I am reading," he told her.

As she did so, she saw more than just a page full of black bugs. She noticed that the letters were in groups, and she knew some of them. Of course she could not yet put them into words, but a feeling of accomplishment surged through her being.

Nathan began at Psalm One. "Blessed is the man—"

"What does that mean?"

"What?"

"Blessed."

After a few seconds' thought, Nathan said, "I suppose it means very happy." Then he began again. "Blessed is the man that walks not in the council of the ungodly."

She was not sure she understood "ungodly" so she interrupted again.

"They are the men and women who do not live the way God wants," Nathan explained.

On they went, taking about a half hour to get through the six short verses of the Psalm. The girl seemed to absorb the entire passage, but was concerned about the contrast between the godly and ungodly person. "The way of the ungodly shall perish" must refer to the Arapaho and Pawnee, she reasoned. Down deep in her mind was a nagging question that she refused to voice. Was she also one of the ungodly? How does God determine who is godly or ungodly? There was much she had to learn.

When Nathan closed the Bible, he told her he was going to pray. She closed her eyes and bowed her head when Nathan did, but shortly thereafter looked up at him as he prayed. She looked all around the cabin to see if the white man's God was there to listen. When she saw nothing unusual, she again bowed her head and closed her eyes. Her mind was too full of questions to hear what her friend was saying until she heard the "Amen."

At that she jumped for the water buckets and headed for the river. Nathan did the morning chores and was out by the horses when the wet Tachechana returned. Quickly she put the buckets at the dry sink and came out to the horse shed where she found Nathan brushing Rowdy.

The water trough at the corral was almost dry and Nathan told Tachechana to bring the water from the house. When he poured one bucket into the trough, he saw a leak and packed it first with some stringy bark and then some cloth that he soaked in warm pine pitch. Then the other bucket was emptied into the trough and they both went to the river to refill them.

Along the way Nathan pointed to some blackberries ripening on the hillside. When they had watered the horses, Nathan fetched two pans from the cabin and they went back after the berries.

All the way to the river and back Nathan would ask, "What is this?" and Tachechana would reply.

They had only been picking a few minutes when Tachechana hooted like an owl. Nathan was startled.

"Tachechana?"

"Hush!" she whispered.

Then he saw her flattened out in the blackberry briars. "What is it?" he whispered.

"Look here!"

Very cautiously he moved over to where the girl was now on her hands and knees. There in the soft earth were moccasin tracks, too big for Tachechana's and too small for his own.

He looked toward the cabin. It could be clearly seen from where the owner of these moccasins stood.

"Indian," said Nathan, nodding to the toes which were pointed straight in front of the heels. "A white man walks with his toes pointed out."

"Eagle Feather," Tachechana affirmed and placed a finger on a distinctive V-shaped notch cut in the sole of the right foot. "He is after me, or my horse." They both looked at the horse shed. Rowdy and The Fox were in the corral contentedly eating the rich grass.

"Let's go back to the cabin and get my rifle," suggested Nathan.

"You get your rifle. I am in no danger from Eagle Feather. He fears the wrath of my father too much to harm me. He might try to kill you to get to me. Go!"

When Nathan returned with both his rifle and revolver, Tachechana had followed the tracks to where Eagle Feather had hidden himself the previous day. Together they tracked him back to where his horse had been tied. From there he had ridden off to the north.

They quickly picked enough berries to eat with their evening meal and returned to the cabin, unaware that Eagle Feather was off visiting the Arapaho camp. It sobered them both to realize that their cabin was no longer a secret to at least one Indian.

Some of the new words added to Tachechana's vocabulary that day were *bullets, powder, primer caps,* and *sights.* Nathan felt uneasy as she repeated these new words. New questions were forming in his mind. If it came to a fight with the Sioux, would Tachechana still consider him a friend? Would she fight against her own people to help him? That would be asking a lot from anyone.

"Tachechana."

"Yes."

"You think Eagle Feather would attack me?"

"He would kill you if he had the chance."

"What would you do if he and I should fight?"

"I would kill him."

"But he is one of your people."

"He would make me his squaw if he could."

"And what is so bad about being a squaw?"

The girl thought for a moment. "Being a squaw is not bad," she said. "But being forced to be a squaw is bad. I do not want to have to be someone's squaw. I will marry when I choose to."

"You do the work of a squaw here."

"I choose to do it here, but I am not a squaw!" Her eyes raged like a storm. "You are my friend. My white man friend. It is the way of the white man that friends work together." Her tone softened somewhat. "My mother was white. My father says there is much of her in me. She did not become his squaw when he captured her. She became his squaw when—"

"She loved him," Nathan concluded.

"I still do not know what love is, but my father said they were very happy together." The finality with which she made that statement led the trapper to drop the subject.

Nathan walked to where the old muzzle loader hung and took it down from the wall. From the shelf he took a powder flask, and a possibles bag, the leather pouch which contained anything a gunman might need. Tachechana followed him as he walked out of the cabin and between the rails of the corral fence.

About seventy-five yards behind the cabin was a wooden frame that formed a box about two feet square. Hanging in the center of this frame was a piece of heavy iron about five inches in diameter.

Nathan told Tachechana to watch closely as he loaded and fired the gun. Carefully he measured out the charge of powder and poured it into the barrel. "Ninety grains," he said. He took the ramrod from its holders beneath the barrel and gently packed the powder inside the barrel. From his possibles bag he took a small piece of cloth that looked like the mattress ticking on her bed. He laid the cloth over the muzzle of the gun and took out a lead ball. Carefully he placed the ball on the cloth patch and with a small wooden tool, called a ball setter, he pushed the ball into the barrel flush with the muzzle. Again he dug into his possibles bag and took out the blade of an old straight razor. With it he cut off the remaining cloth from around the muzzle, and pushed the ball and its patch down the barrel with the ramrod.

He looked at the girl. Her attention never left him. Once again he placed a cap on the muzzle loader's nipple and told Tachechana it was now ready to fire. She didn't quite understand so he showed her how to draw back the hammer and told her that when he pulled the trigger the gun would go off. He brought the old gun to his cheek almost lovingly and aligned the sights on the steel disk. The gun went off with a roar that startled the girl, but she smiled when she heard the distinct clank of the lead ball hitting the disk.

They both dropped to their knees to see below the blue-gray smoke. Sure enough the disk was swinging back and forth from the impact of the ball.

"Would you like to try it now?" he asked.

She nearly jumped up and down with excitement. He let her hold the gun upright as he went through the loading process. She had remembered every step except the "ninety grains" of powder. She didn't know what "ninety" was. Nathan knew he would have to teach her arithmetic, too.

The gun was a rather heavy .54 caliber, and Nathan wasn't sure she could hold it up, but if she was willing to try, he was willing to let her. He explained the principle of sighting and told her to hold it with both hands and against her shoulder and her cheek.

She did as she was told, but when the gun went off, dirt flew about six feet in front and to the right of the target. She was disappointed, but Nathan reassured her that it was a good first effort.

"Don't pull on the trigger," he told her. "Squeeze it gently, then the ball will go where you want it."

Again she held the gun while he loaded it. This time she squeezed the trigger gently, but again there was no resounding clang as the ball met the target. They walked down to the disk and saw where her second shot had just missed.

"Let me try again!" the eager girl shouted.

This time Nathan let her do everything but measure the powder. Carefully she aligned the sights, took a deep breath, and squeezed the trigger. The rifle roared, the target clanged, and girl and man both whooped.

To his surprise and chagrin, he found himself hugging the girl and she was hugging back. Then, stiffly, Nathan pulled away, but he didn't try to hide the joy in his eyes over her accomplishment.

The day's shooting lesson did not end when they returned to the cabin. Nathan took down the cleaning kit and showed her the proper way to clean and oil the fine old weapon. As he replaced it on its peg on the wall, he wondered uneasily if he had been wise to shoot the old gun. Any nearby Indian would surely hear it. Could also be a warning to stay away, he concluded.

Eagle Feather was not yet back to his camp when he heard the gunfire. Had he made a mistake in going after the Arapaho arrows? *Did Running Coyote find them, too?* he wondered.

Tomorrow he would again scout out the trapper's cabin to discover what had happened and, if possible, kill the trapper. Tonight, however, he would risk building a fire to have a warm meal of rabbit caught in one of his snare traps. There was no wind and the smoke would rise and dissipate before it could give away his position.

Inside the trapper's cabin Nathan was preparing the last of his venison. "Tomorrow we will have to hunt for more meat," he told her.

"Then I will teach you how to shoot a bow to kill deer," she said with a smile.

After supper, Nathan gave Tachechana two sheets of paper with the rest of the alphabet on it. "This is the last of the letters you must learn before you begin to learn words," he told her.

"Will I then be able to read?"

"No, but soon."

Nathan realized that they were speaking more English now than Sioux. Verbs were still a problem, but she would soon learn them.

He took down his Bible and began to read. Every once in a while he would glance up to find a pair of green eyes looking at him. They would both smile and go back to work.

Finally, she handed him her paper. It was covered with the last of the alphabet. She could recite it all from memory.

Later Nathan lay on his bed, thinking of the great change that had taken place in his life in only ten days.

Let Not Your Heart Be Troubled

Chapter

10

EAGLE FEATHER WAS NOT THE ONLY ONE to hear Tachechana's target practice. Far to the east Running Coyote
reined his horse to an abrupt halt and cupped his hand
behind his half-gone ear. The echoes of the shots off the
stone walls behind the cabin made it hard for him to detect
from where they were coming.

Sure that they came from west of his position and were
probably fired by the trapper, he swung his horse in that
general direction. When he got to the river and made his
camp for the night, he had no way of knowing that he was
within a mile of Eagle Feather's camp.

Nathan and Tachechana were up before daylight the next
morning preparing to ride into the hills to shoot a deer for
their meat supply. After breakfast they were about to
mount their horses when Tachechana remembered something and told Nathan to wait. She ran back into the cabin
and came out with two flat, red, sandstone rocks about two
inches in diameter. She spit on one of them and began
grinding the other into the spittle. In only a few seconds
she had a red brown paste which she took, and with a small
stick, drew the outline of a deer on her right forearm.

She put the stones on one of the fence posts and threw herself up on the waiting back of Fox.

"Why did you do that?" Nathan asked.

"It is a prayer," she said, being careful to use one of her new English words properly. "It is how we ask the Great Spirit to guide us on the hunt and make our arrows fly true."

Nathan first smiled, then frowned. He knew the Sioux to be a religious people, but their religion was superstition and a worship of the creation rather than the Creator. But then he felt a check. Maybe God would honor this kind of written prayer as much as He would a spoken one.

They rode in silence for almost an hour, searching the ground for the heart-shaped tracks of deer, and scanning the brush around them for that patch of brown hair, a black nose, or the uneven shape of antler that would betray the deer.

As they got to the more broken part of the hills, both the hunters became more alert. Nathan had decided he would let Tachechana try to kill the first deer they saw, but he kept his rifle out of its scabbard and lying across the saddle in front of him. They were in grizzly country and he wanted to be prepared for any eventuality. Nor had he forgotten the moccasin tracks they found the day before.

Just as they topped one hill, out jumped the first deer. Both hunters reined as the animal sped up the next hill with the stiff-legged bounds typical of mule deer. At the very top of that hill he stopped and looked back at them.

Tachechana turned her horse around and started back down the hill.

"Come!" she said.

Nathan wanted badly to shoot at it across the small valley, but this was her show. He turned Rowdy and followed her.

As soon as she was sure the deer could no longer see them, she dismounted and tied Fox to a sagebrush. Nathan did the same.

"You wait here," she said and slipped quietly through the brush toward a position where she could ambush the deer. Nathan followed stealthily at a distance, determined to see her in action.

Tachechana had circled the first hill and was now headed around the second. She seemed to know just about where the deer would be. The trapper watched in admiration as the girl moved through the sagebrush and cactus like a ghost.

The deer never heard her as she came around the hill below him. When she was about thirty yards away, she took an arrow from her quiver and rolled it over the image of a deer she had sketched on her forearm. She nocked the arrow in the sinew string of her bow and drew it to its full length.

The deer heard the twang of the bow, but before he could spring to his feet the arrow caught him cleanly in the rib cage just behind the front leg. Though his lungs were shredded by the arrow, he still got up and ran down the hill past Tachechana and about another sixty or seventy yards, before he toppled over dead.

It had taken the arrow less than ten seconds to kill the big buck.

Nathan waited until she gave the hoot of an owl before he brought Rowdy and Fox to the site of the kill.

The deer was sprawled out, the arrow still in his chest. Nathan's grin was surpassed only by Tachechana's.

As the animals got close to the fallen game and Rowdy smelled the blood, he began to shy and rear. Fox, on the other hand, walked right up to the carcass. This was nothing new to her.

When Tachechana pulled the bloody arrow from the deer, she rubbed it over the sketch of the deer on her forearm. She was extra careful to see that every mark of the drawing was covered with blood so that none of it could be seen.

Without being told, Nathan knew this was the Sioux method of thanking the Great Spirit for a successful hunt. She later explained it also was to show the spirit of the deer that Tachechana had no malice toward the animal and that she was sorry she had to kill him for food.

As they began to field dress the animal, Nathan was in for more surprises. Normally, when gutting out an animal, he took only the best of the meat, figuring that coyotes and vultures would devour what was left. Tachechana would have none of that. She built a fire upon which she placed the lungs, stomach, and intestines. As the smoke ascended she did a toe-heel dance step around the fire to thank the Great Spirit again for their successful hunt.

Rowdy had a major fit of bucking and rearing as Nathan prepared to tie the deer carcass behind the saddle. Finally Nathan took off his vest and had Tachechana hold it over Rowdy's eyes while the deer was placed on the horse's back. Nathan took special care to see to it that the antlers of the deer could not slide down and gore the horse.

Fox, on the other hand, watched indifferently as the sack

containing the deer's heart, liver, and kidneys was thrown over her back. Being a war horse, the smell of blood was exciting to her. Besides, Fox's role in life was to please the little Indian girl who loved her so.

Eagle Feather was surprised to find the cabin empty when he arrived at his hiding place. He was also disturbed to find other tracks on top of his. The girl and the trapper knew he was there. Now his task would be even harder.

When he backtracked to his horse and circled the area carefully, he discovered their tracks going off to the southwest. Instead of following them, he wiped out his own tracks with a handful of brush and circled around to the north of the cabin. After tying his horse in a thick stand of trees, he climbed the hill overlooking the cabin.

There was no way for him to get down the sheer rock face to the cabin, but it was a good place to watch what was happening there. He had only been in his new hiding place a short time when he saw Nathan and Tachechana round the south hill and ride up to the horse shed. He noted the deer carcass and, having heard no gunfire, concluded that Tachechana had made the kill. He smiled and thought to himself, *The white man has not turned the girl's thinking. She is still a hunter, not a squaw.*

Upon arrival back at the cabin, Nathan retrieved three long poles from the rafters of the horse shed. They were tied together at one end with the other ends spread out like a three pointed star. The main carcass of the deer was brought to the center of the star and a gambrel was placed in the tendon that ran down the back of the rear leg. The gambrel was tied to the rope holding the poles together. Nathan then went to the outer edge of one of the points of the star and pushed it toward the center, lifting the deer a little off the ground. He repeated this with each pole until the deer was hanging in a head down position for draining and cooling.

Tachechana meanwhile was slicing some of the liver for frying. When Nathan saw her intention, he strode down by the river and pulled some wild onions to mix with the liver.

Later both Nathan and Tachechana strolled down to the river with water buckets. Carefully they washed the blood and hair from their hands. On the way back Nathan held a bucket in his right hand and shared the load in his left hand with her. The difference in their size made some of the water splash on Tachechana. She let out a little squealing giggle and then splashed water on him. They both laughed.

Tachechana suddenly became serious. Nathan wondered what was wrong but said nothing. He could not know that she was remembering the words of her father concerning himself and her mother. "We laughed much together." She missed her father, but being a Sioux warrior, she could not admit it.

Throughout the day Running Coyote was still trying to locate the origin of the shooting he heard the day before. For a while he rode to the north on the east side of the river. Convinced the sound could not have come from that far north, he crossed the river and started south. He stopped when he came to the stream where Nathan and Tachechana had caught the trout. He noticed the tracks left by Eagle Feather, and without thinking ran his fingers over the bright scar on his right cheek. Since the horse was unshod he knew it was that of an Indian. None of the Indians from his village had a gun, so he felt safe following the tracks.

Since he was one of the best trackers in the tribe, it didn't take him long to find Eagle Feather's camp. He knew that Eagle Feather had found Tachechana or he would not have made so permanent a camp.

Running Coyote was careful to cover his tracks as he moved up the stream a ways where he could watch for the return of Eagle Feather. Soon now he would have the girl's great horse as his own. With Fox he would be able to outrun Great Bear. It would not be long before he would be Chief Running Coyote. He settled in under a low growing spruce tree to continue his vigil.

Inside the trapper's cabin Nathan and Tachechana were in a festive mood. When the cooking fire was ready, liver, onions, and the leftover cattail potatoes were all fried in the same pan. Coffee was boiling on the back of the stove and Nathan fixed his best biscuit recipe.

They sat at the table and, without being told, she bowed her head and closed her eyes before starting to eat. Nathan thanked God for providing the fresh meat and other good things for their bodies and asked for wisdom for the days ahead.

At the word "Amen," Tachechana dug into the food with a passion. The work and excitement of the day had given her a tremendous appetite. As she ate, Nathan had a good feeling about their unusual friendship. He recalled their conversation about the word "love" two nights previous, and knew in a way he did love her. Not romantic love, of course. A father-daughter type of love, he decided. He wondered how she really felt about him.

"Since I now know all the letters, will you teach me words tonight?" she asked.

"We will try."

She was so excited about getting started that she helped him get the dishes to the dry sink and poured water over them.

"If you are not careful you will become a squaw," Nathan said with a grin.

"When I learn to read I will not have to be a squaw. I will be a lady."

Nathan had used the word *lady* around her only once or twice. Most of the time he used *woman*. He marveled at how quickly she took the word and figured out the subtle difference.

"What is the difference between *woman* and *lady*?" he asked.

"The squaws are women. My mother was a lady." Defiance and resolve sparkled in her eyes.

"And you want to be like your mother?"

"I *will* be like my mother."

"Then we had better get you started on your reading and writing." He went to the shelf that held his tablet and pencil stub. "We will start with your name. I will tell you the letter and you write it on the paper."

She readied herself.

"T."

Tt she wrote.

"No, just the tall 'T,'" he corrected. She made a T.
"Small A."

By the time she got to the second "a" of her name she
was beginning to despair. Frustration showed on her face
and she began to forget what the letters looked like. She
was getting more and more angry with herself.

"Tachechana?"

"What?"

"Your name is a long one, and difficult to write. It is a
pretty name to say and it sounds like a song. But if it were
shorter, it would be easier to write."

"What would you call me?"

"Chana."

"Chana doesn't mean anything. Tachechana means 'Skipping Fawn.'"

"I know, but Nathan doesn't mean anything either. You
know who I am when I say Nathan. People will know who
you are when they say Chana."

"But I am Tachechana."

"You will always be Tachechana, but to write it is hard.
Chana would be easy. And Chana has a nice sound to it,
doesn't it?"

"Chana," she said, "Chana! Yes, I will be Chana when I
write, but my father will always know me as Tachechana."

"And I will, too."

Nathan took down the book with the illustration of a
horse and pointed to the word *horse* under it.

She spelled it out correctly and Nathan told her to write
it. She did, with a smile of achievement.

Nathan found five or six other short words for her to

learn that night. By the time she had them all memorized it was time for bed.

"You did not read God's words yet," she protested when Nathan suggested it was late. With a smile he took down the Bible, and opened it to John 1 and read aloud:

"In the beginning was the Word, and the Word was with God, and the Word was God. The same was in the beginning with God. All things were made by him; and without him was not anything made that was made."

As Nathan paused the girl asked, "Can words make things?"

This was the response for which Nathan had hoped. Since she was looking at the words as he read, he pointed down to verse fourteen and read: "And the Word was made flesh, and dwelt among us, (and we beheld his glory, the glory as of the only begotten of the Father,) full of grace and truth."

As best he could, Nathan explained how God sent Jesus to live and die on the earth so that all men could go to heaven when they die.

"Is heaven the other world where my mother is waiting for my father?"

"God's Book has much to say about heaven and how we get to go there."

"My father said my mother is waiting for him there. She is there."

"She may very well be, but if she is—"

"She *is*!"

"Then it is because she loves Jesus."

"I do not understand!" the girl said as she got up and went to her room.

As the blanket door dropped behind her, Nathan let out a big sigh. "This is going to be a much bigger job than I thought," he mumbled to himself. Then he prayed, not for himself as was his custom, but for the soul of this savage girl who had come to mean so much to him.

Chapter

11

IN THE SECURITY OF HER SMALL ROOM Tachechana could not sleep. *Why would Nathan question what my father said about my mother?* she thought. *What does a white man's Jesus have to do with the spirit of an Indian?* But she also remembered her mother was white, and that made her at least part white. Did she not have green eyes?

Questions came that no amount of reasoning could solve. Was the white man's heaven and the Indian Spirit World really the same? If they were not, how would her father see her mother again? And what would happen to her since she was neither red nor white?

She had never even thought of questioning the word of her father. He would not, could not, lie to her. Nathan would have no reason to lie to her either. Why should he? He was her friend. Where then was the truth? With these questions burning in her mind, she finally fell into troubled sleep.

Nathan, on the other side of the blanket door, also had many unanswerable questions. He was used to such uncertainty, but since making his peace with God he was learning more patience both with himself and his circumstances. As he contemplated his companion in the next room he had an inner assurance that God was about to do something great on her behalf. Already she had been the instrument for his restoration. In quiet assurance he fell asleep.

As the sun rose through a misty fog, Eagle Feather picked his way to the perch on the north cliff overlooking the cabin. He had no idea that Running Coyote had observed his return the day before and was now watching his every move, as well as the cabin, from a nearby hiding place.

The first activity both Indians saw was a wisp of smoke curling from the chimney. Then Nathan appeared in front of the cabin and walked to where the deer had been hung the day before. The tripod affair they used to hang the animal was under a large yellow pine tree which the sun could not penetrate.

Carefully Nathan peeled back the skin on one hind leg and cut out two choice steaks. After pulling the skin back over the remaining portions of the leg, he took the steak inside for breakfast.

If this were the pattern the trapper would follow for the next few days, thought Eagle Feather, *it might be possible for me to get close enough to the deer while still dark to ambush him when he comes out.*

Running Coyote was able to surmise what Eagle Feather was planning. Yet both Indians noticed that the trapper now carried a revolver in a holster hung low at his side.

Back inside the cabin Nathan found Chana up and going over her new words with her usual industry.

"Can we do words this morning?"

"There are chores that must be done."

"The deer can hang for one more day before we tan the hide."

"But we must gather some grass for the horses. They have to eat when the snow is on the ground."

This was a new thought to Tachechana. Indian horses were left to pasture all winter. "How can you save grass?" she asked. "No one saves grass for the wild horses and they survive."

"Haven't you noticed how strong the white man's horses are in the spring, and how thin and weak the Indian's horses are?"

"Yes."

"That is because the white man dries grass in the summer and feeds it to his horses all winter."

For the first time Tachechana realized that all white men, and not Nathan alone, really cared for their horses.

"Must we do that today?"

"Yes. It's a dry time. We must dry grass into hay and venison into jerky."

If drying grass was good for the horses, Tachechana favored it. After breakfast Nathan produced a scythe from the horse shed and walked into the west pasture where the grass was at its best.

At first Tachechana thought the slow, swinging gait of Nathan to be quite comical. The smooth swath of grass he left behind soon made her understand the process of "making hay" as Nathan called it.

When Nathan stopped for a rest or drink of water, Tachechana picked up the scythe and tried her hand at it. She couldn't seem to get the necessary rhythm or length of the stroke. Gladly she gave the scythe back to Nathan each time he came near her.

Tachechana soon lost interest in making hay and went to tend the horses in the corral. She took down Nathan's brushes and began to brush the horses, her thoughts turning to the village and her father. She missed him very much, but knew she must not return. Not yet. When she did she would have learned to read, and would be a lady like her mother.

As Nathan worked he thought of all the things that must be done in the near future. His catch of beaver must be taken to the trader. He must lay in more firewood for winter. His traps must be checked and ready for the new season. His potatoes and squash harvested and stored. And, most of all, Tachechana must learn to read.

Nathan had more than half the field cut when he realized the shadows were getting longer and his stomach needed nourishment. He would finish cutting early enough the next day to begin preparation for his trip to the trader the day after.

He carried the scythe back to the horse shed and hung it in the rafters.

"You have made the horses look very good," he told the girl.

"They like being brushed."

"I'm sure they do. It tells them you love them."

Tachechana giggled.

"What is so funny?"

"Nothing," she said and giggled again as she headed for the cabin door with an arm load of firewood.

Nathan stood and watched her lighthearted tread as she entered the door. He shook his head. "I don't think I'll ever understand that girl!" He walked over to the deer carcass and cut two more steaks. This time he cut them larger than usual. Mowing the hay had given him a large appetite.

By the time Nathan got inside the cabin Tachechana already was building the fire. The trapper surmised that she was not only hungry but that she was eager for supper to be over so she could learn more words.

As Nathan scraped the carrots before putting them in the pan, he broke off a piece and popped it raw into his mouth.

Tachechana saw the action and suddenly appeared by his side. Smiling, he broke off another piece and popped it into her eager mouth. She crunched it with delight and opened her mouth for more. But Nathan dropped the rest into the pan with the partially cooked meat.

When the food was prepared and both were sitting at the table, Nathan asked, "Would you like to thank God for our food tonight?"

The girl looked horror stricken. "I don't know what to say."

"Just thank God for what He has given us," he urged.

"No, I don't think the Great Sp—God listens to women."

"I'm sure He does."

"No," she said as she looked at her plate like a very shy little girl.

"All right, I'll pray." And he did. He asked God for protection and realized he was full of fear.

Not much was said as the meal started. Nathan finally broke the silence. "How do you like the carrots?"

"Like them better raw."

"Your teeth must be better than mine."

She giggled.

"You know an old horse's teeth get worn down with age. Old horses and old men are alike."

Nathan felt a sudden pang. The rest of the meal was eaten in silence.

After the dishes had been washed, they sat down at the table to begin the evening lesson on words.

Tachechana had something on her mind. "Love must be something very special," she began.

"It is."

"How can I know what it is?"

"What is most important to you?"

"Fox."

"What else?"

"Learning to read and write."

"Anything else?"

"My father, the Chief."

"Let's start with these then. How do you feel about Fox?"

"I am happy when she is near. I feel strong when we gallop over the prairie."

"What about reading and writing?"

"When I can read and write, I will be like my mother. My father will be proud of me. The village will respect me."

"How do you feel about your father?"

"Proud. He is wise and strong. He cared for me when I was just a baby after my mother went to the Spirit W—to heaven."

"Go over the things you've just said," Nathan said. "Love makes you feel happy and strong. It makes you want to be proud and be respected. It makes you feel cared for."

"Is that all?"

"No, there is much more. It is a feeling deep within you that makes you . . . feel good to be with another person."

"Do I love you, Nathan?"

"No! You can't love me; I am so much older than you."

"But I feel about you all of the things you say is love."

"Respect is very much like love." He was struggling. "You respect me as you would the Elders of your village."

"I don't know."

"We better get to your reading lessons."

Knowing she was weak on her verbs, he gave her a list of ten: walk, run, jump, ride, hunt, talk, listen, see, smell, and do. He made sure she could put the right word with the right action and told her to write a line of each word on the paper.

After completing his evening chores, he took down a book to read. He scanned the pages briefly, but could find nothing that could hold his interest. He put up that book and took down another with the same results.

Finally he took down his Bible. The pages fell open to John 14.

"Let not your heart be troubled: ye believe in God, believe also in me. In my Father's house are many mansions: if it were not so, I would have told you. I go to prepare a place for you. And if I go and prepare a place for you, I will come again and receive you unto myself; that where I am, there ye may be also. . . . Peace I leave with you, my peace I give unto you. . . . Let not your heart be troubled, neither let it be afraid."

123

The Scripture did its work in his heart. He was no longer so concerned for the safety of the girl and himself. He felt so relaxed he smiled warmly at Tachechana.

"What has happened?" the girl asked.

"What do you mean?"

"You have changed since supper. You are no longer . . . as you were before."

"I have been worried about the one you call Eagle Feather."

"Do you fear him?"

"I did until a few moments ago."

"What changed you? Was it something God said in His Book?"

"Yes, He said He would give me peace."

"That's good," she said, and handed him her paper. Every line was duplicated as Nathan had told her. He asked her to say each word and define it as best she could. She had every one of them correct.

"You are doing very well!"

She smiled her appreciation.

"We had better get to bed. It's getting late."

"Nathan. . . ."

"Yes?"

"When will you teach me *love*?"

He wrote the word on a piece of paper and said, "This is the word *love*, but its meaning you must learn for yourself. I don't know how to teach you other than what we said before."

Her disappointment showed on her face, but she didn't press him further. She took her papers to her room with her as always.

Soon the candle in her room was out and the oil lamp in the larger room followed suit. They both slept the sleep of peace.

It was just before first light when Rowdy whinnied. Both were awake at once, listening. They heard nothing and soon fell back to sleep.

Shortly after the sun cracked the eastern horizon Nathan opened the cabin door. As usual he scanned every rock and bush before committing himself to the light. He walked the path to the outhouse then back to the cabin where he washed his hands and came back out to carve the breakfast meat.

Nathan carefully inspected the carcass of the deer, turning his back on the sagebrush where a stealthy figure was poised. As he prepared to make a cut, Nathan dropped the knife.

"Clumsy!" he said out loud as he bent to pick it up.

Then, as Nathan began again to cut the venison, the figure raised his bow. Suddenly fingers of iron covered his mouth, and sharp steel was pressed to his throat.

Slowly Eagle Feather sank back into the brush. The strong hand that held him permitted him to turn enough to see the cruel face of Running Coyote. Eagle Feather lay there with the knife at his throat until Nathan finished his task and returned to the cabin.

Only then did Running Coyote break the silence.

"I could have killed you," he whispered to Eagle Feather. "But you are a brother. The girl and her horse are mine. You will go and tell that to all the braves of the village or you will die. Do you understand?"

Eagle Feather nodded his head and the fingers of iron were released from his mouth. The knife remained at his throat.

"I, too, would like the girl," said Eagle Feather.

"If I see you near here again I will kill you."

"I will go."

"You will go and tell the village the girl and her horse are mine."

Eagle Feather nodded again and Running Coyote slowly released the pressure of the knife on his throat. They both looked at the cabin door. It was shut and they were safe to steal away.

Chapter
12

INSIDE THE CABIN neither Nathan nor Tachechana knew how close Nathan had been to death, or that Running Coyote should be the one to save his life.

Nathan dawdled over his breakfast this morning. The girl could tell that his back ached from the work of the previous day.

Tachechana, on the other hand, was anxious to get the haying done so she could spend more time learning her words.

"Why are you taking so long with your food?" she asked.

"There is too much dew on the grass to mow it now," was the half-true answer.

"Will you be finished with it today?"

"It will all be cut today. After it dries for two or three days, we will gather it up and stack it near the horse shed."

"While it is drying can we study more words?"

"Tomorrow I will give you many words to study while I go to the trader with my furs."

"The trader?"

"Yes, we need some supplies, and if I don't trade my beaver furs soon they will not be worth as much."

"I will go to the trader, too."

"It would not be safe for you there."

"I am a warrior, I am safe everywhere."

"You had better stay here."

"I *will* go!" She remembered her father telling her how her mother followed him to the trader once and how she would speak to the trader in the Sioux tongue.

In spite of her defiance to Nathan, she had a smile on her face. *There is much of my mother in me,* she thought.

Nathan let out a sigh and shrugged his shoulders, "First we must cut the grass."

Tachechana sprang from the table to the water buckets. One was still half-full so she poured it into the basin, splashing some on the dry sink and herself. She then headed out the door and to the river.

Nathan had straightened up the main room of the cabin and was running the sharpening stone over the blade of the scythe when Tachechana returned with the two buckets full of water. The wet spots on her shirt and breeches confirmed the usual morning swim, and always brought a smile to Nathan's face.

For the first hour of work Tachechana walked right behind Nathan. She somehow thought that action would make the job go faster. All it did was make Nathan nervous.

"Why don't you see if you can get us a couple grouse for supper?" he suggested.

The idea delighted her. She ran back to the cabin and got her bow and several arrows with small, fine heads. She bounded out of the cabin and around the hill to the south where there was a stand of stately spruce trees.

Once in the shade of the trees she stopped and listened. Her eyes were everywhere at once. Hearing and seeing no grouse, she took a few steps and froze again. The process was repeated several times before she saw the grouse looking at her from a low limb.

Carefully she drew the bow the full length of the arrow and released it. The arrow struck the bird in the crop, just where neck and breast came together. Happily she ran to the dead bird and picked it up. The arrow had gone right through and she saw it was a clean kill.

Being a true hunter she was a bit sad that one of the wild creatures had to die in order to meet her needs. She smoothed out the ruffled feathers before she cinched its head in her sash belt.

After finding her arrow stuck in a nearby tree, she carved it free with her knife, and again started her hunt for another bird. Stop, look, listen, proceed. Stop, look, listen, proceed. It took her almost an hour before she saw the second bird.

This time her arrow was deflected by an unnoticed twig between her and the grouse. It always annoyed her when that happened, but she felt a clean miss was the only alternative to a clean kill.

When an arrow was deflected by a twig it could scoot in most any direction. After diligent search she finally found it almost buried in the spruce needles of the forest floor.

By the time she found and killed a second bird, Nathan had almost finished the mowing. Proudly she held up the two birds as she rounded the corner of the horse shed. He smiled and waved, "By the time you pluck the feathers I'll be finished."

She nodded and went to the pit where Nathan put his garbage. It took her but a few moments to remove the feathers, heads, and feet from the two birds. These were put in the pit, but the entrails were put in a jar and buried where she had seen Nathan bury similar jars.

Nathan came up just as she finished covering it with dirt.

"Good!" he exclaimed with pride.

"Why do you bury these parts of birds and rabbits?"

"Soon the fox and coyote furs will be prime. Then we will use these parts to bait our traps."

Tachechana was pleased to hear him say "*our* traps." He was including her in more and more of his life.

While she gathered firewood and built a fire, Nathan went into the cabin to make some of his famous biscuits.

When the grouse were cooked to her satisfaction, she carried them into the cabin where Nathan had everything else ready. On the table were warm biscuits, a bowl of raw carrots in water, and beside each of their plates a bowl containing a biscuit covered with blackberries.

There was something so festive about this meal they took their time eating. When Tachechana told of her miss on the second shot, she stuck out her lower lip like a pouting child and puffed out a little puff of air. Something about her expression delighted Nathan and he burst out laughing. Quickly she joined him.

When Tachechana began to eat her blackberry shortcake she was doubly surprised. They were the sweetest berries she had ever eaten.

"I put the last of the sugar on them," said Nathan. "A special treat for the hunter that supplied the meat. Tomorrow we get fresh supplies."

After supper Nathan listed some new words for her: "Trade, trader." Here he had to explain the difference between the two. "Fur, food, eat, sleep, cook, fire, cup, and fork." She began with her usual diligence to print the words.

The following morning the girl and the trapper were up before daybreak to get an early start to the trading post. Tachechana, however, found time to race down to the river for her morning swim.

From his vantage point on the cliff Running Coyote noted with interest her morning habit. He grinned when he saw her undress to swim. It seemed to him she had grown in the weeks since the council fire. *She will make a fine squaw, indeed,* he thought.

As she carried the water buckets back to the cabin, his eyes searched every step she took. He was thinking of ways to kidnap her from Nathan, and persuade her, one way or another, to be his squaw. He would have her and her horse yet.

With the beaver pelts firmly secured on Rowdy and Fox, Nathan led the way to the river and headed south to a spot where the river was shallow enough for them to cross without getting the furs wet. Then they took an easterly direction.

In a way, Nathan was glad to have Tachechana's company, but he was dreading the word of *his* squaw being passed up and down the prairie and through the mountains, as it was sure to do when the people at the trading post saw her. How silly to think that a man as old as he would become involved with a young Indian girl. Yet he did not like to think what life in the cabin would be like without her.

"How far is it to the trader's?" asked Chana.

"It will take us most of the day to get there."

"Will there be other white men there?"

"Yes."

"White women, too?"

"Yes."

"If the white men and the Indians both trade at the same place, why do they not kill each other there?"

"Since both whites and Indians need the trader, they have decided there will be no fighting there. If someone starts to fight, the trader will not trade with him anymore."

They both knew that Indians in the past had attacked and burned several trading posts. Each time this happened soldiers, in turn, had massacred an Indian village.

"If all men can get along at the trader's, why can't they get along everywhere?" asked Tachechana.

"It is for everyone's good that there be no fighting at the trader's, but in the mountains, and on the prairie evil men, both red and white, look only for what is good for themselves."

"What makes some men evil?"

Nathan thought about that question for a long time before answering.

"God's Book says that all men are basically evil."

"Even my father the Chief?"

"It says all men."

"Even you?"

"Yes."

"But not my mother."

"It says all men and women."

"I don't think I like your Bible."

Again Nathan paused.

"Are you an evil person?" he finally asked.

"No." Her answer was subdued and somewhat shaken.

"Have you ever done anything for which you were sorry?"

"No!" This time there was resolution in her voice. "The Sioux are a noble people."

"So are many white men."

"Then why does your God call them evil?"

Nathan worried that he might be driving her away with this basic Christian theology.

"Do you think me evil?"

"No," was her quick reply.

"But you know I have done evil things."

"What is done is done. You are now good."

"That doesn't change the fact about my basic nature." He paused a moment, "What happened with the second grouse you shot at yesterday?"

"My arrow hit a twig and bounced away from the bird."

"Was your bow strong enough?"

"Yes."

"Was your aim true?"

"Yes!"

"Still you missed the bird because something got in the way. The twig that deflected your arrow was there all the time, but you didn't see it. It is the same with our aim to be good people. Even when we do our best we miss sometimes because there is an evil twig in us that makes us do wrong things."

"What wrong things did my mother do?"

"I never knew your mother, but I know you. You get very angry at times, like the night you drove your tomahawk into my table."

"Is it wrong to be angry?"

"Was it right for you to chop my table?"

"No ... but ..."

"There are many things that make God unhappy."

At that point in their conversation Rowdy, who had been leading the way, shied and backed into Fox who took a nip at his hindquarters. There in front of them lay a large diamondback rattlesnake.

Nathan was about to draw his six gun and kill the snake when Tachechana said, "No!"

She slid from her horse's back and with a long stick she encouraged the snake from the trail and out of their way.

"If we killed the snake with no reason the spirit of the snake would tell other snakes to hunt us and kill us."

She remounted and they rode on for some time in silence. Nathan was perplexed. He had no idea how he could get a girl with superstitious beliefs to understand something as straightforward as Scripture. All he could do was silently ask the Spirit of God to work in her heart.

During the last part of the journey, they rode in silence, but Tachechana's mind was busy. Her father had told her the Great Spirit and her mother's God were the same. Nathan said they were, too. Why was there so much difference in what she had learned as an Indian, and what she was now trying to learn as a white woman? Was her problem the fact that she was neither red nor white? If the

Great Spirit, or God, was so good, why did He say she was evil?

She thought back over her life. Could it be that she was not as good as she thought she was? She remembered doing things that now she questioned. She remembered stealing things. She remembered lying. She even remembered disobeying her father and doing things he told her not to do.

The thought of having displeased her father brought storm clouds to her normally radiant eyes. She missed him very much and wanted to tell him she was sorry for not pleasing him as much as she could. The lump that came to her throat the last night she had spent in his tepee was finding its way there again. Her eyes began to sting. She would not permit herself the embarrassment of a tear. She could not.

They topped out over a small hill and there before them lay the trading post. Tachechana was relieved to see it, for now her thoughts could change. She was about to have a new adventure.

Chapter

13

As Tachechana and Nathan approached the stockade, the girl's eyes were ablaze with excitement and curiosity. She had never seen a stockade before. Within the log walls were several buildings. She was surprised to find a group of six or eight tepees set up outside the wall on the west side, and army tents on the east. Here were red men and white men living side by side.

Tachechana studied the tepees. All of them had Sioux markings so she relaxed somewhat, and turned her attention to the army tents. She looked nervously at Nathan.

"Don't worry, you're all right with me here," he told her.

She looked at the stockade. It was really a log fort, but it had only a few men to defend it and no cannon. The only entrance was a gate large enough for a team of horses and a freight wagon to pass. A couple of men with rifles stood at this gate.

As he approached, Nathan was recognized by one of them.

"Well, Nathan, we were wondering if you still had your hair," greeted the taller of the two. His obviously broken nose pointed first east then west. "I see you finally got yourself a squaw."

137

Tachechana's hand gripped her tomahawk.

"She's not my squaw. She's the daughter of Chief Great Bear and she's here to trade her beaver hides," Nathan said and pointed to the furs on the back of the horse.

There was no change on the face of the girl, but she was surprised to hear Nathan say they were her furs.

"Pretty for a half-breed," said the one with the crooked nose.

"You be careful how you talk about one of your boss's customers," Nathan warned.

Tachechana moved Fox right up to Crooked Nose and said in perfect English, "I'm a lady," and led Nathan through the gate and up to the hitching post in front of the store.

The tall gatekeeper stood with his mouth hanging open while his partner was convulsed with laughter. Nathan didn't laugh, but his grin was the biggest Tachechana had ever seen. Evidently her being a lady pleased Nathan.

In front of the store they dismounted, then Nathan removed his hat and made a bowing gesture that insisted she enter first. He quickly followed her through the door, and took her by the elbow and led her to the counter behind which stood a leathery, wizened old man.

"Howdy, Nathan," drawled the trader.

"Hello, Jim. This is Miss Tachechana, daughter of Great Bear. She and I each have some beaver pelts to trade."

"So this is Great Bear's daughter. I coulda told by her eyes. Jus like her ma's."

"You know of my mother?"

"She speaks English," said the trader, turning to Nathan.

"Better than you do."

"When her mamma came in here 'bout eighteen years ago she only spoke Sioux. I ain't seen her since."

"She died when Tachechana was born," Nathan explained.

"What was my mother like?"

"She was white. A mite taller 'n you with brown hair. Pretty, too, just like you."

"What's the army doing here, Jim? You been having trouble?"

"I haven't," Jim replied, "but more and more of the braves are bolting the reservation. They raided a couple of trading posts and are stealing guns.

"The army's tryin' to round them up, but can't seem to find them. Since I carry a good number of guns, they camped here for a while. They're supposed to leave in two or three days."

Nathan looked somber. "I don't blame the Indians for leaving the reservation. Poor land, poor food, no dignity; you or I wouldn't put up with it."

"The captain of this troop says the army is going to send out at least three regiments against the Indians next summer, if they don't get back on the reservation," Jim said.

"Well," Nathan said, "it's getting late. We'd like to get a receipt for our hides and set up camp. We'll come back in the morning and pick up our supplies."

"Sure thing."

They went out to the horses and Nathan motioned for Jim to check out the girl's furs first. Jim was an honest trader, but not quite as honest with Indians as with white men.

"Injuns don't usually care for hides as good as this," Jim said.

"I helped her a bit," Nathan replied.

"I see."

When he finished tallying up the value of the furs, he wrote a crude receipt and handed it to the girl. She studied it carefully and looked over Jim's shoulder to Nathan.

Nathan nodded to her and she nodded to Jim.

"Now let's take a looky at yours."

Nathan untied the bundle of furs that had been behind Rowdy's saddle and laid them on the porch of the store. Nathan's bundle of furs was considerably larger than Tachechana's so the trader began making piles of furs as he graded them. Small, medium, large, and blue or those not in prime. Occasionally Nathan would pick up one from the pile where Jim had laid it and hand it back to him to grade again. Once or twice Jim changed his mind and put it on the next better pile, but most of the time he would show Nathan some supposed fault in the pelt and put it back where it was. It was all part of the trading game.

Nathan, his back to the entrance of the stockade, didn't see the four soldiers coming his way. They were about to enter the store when Nathan turned. The eldest of the soldiers, a captain, stopped in midstride and looked sharply into Nathan's face.

"Cooper!" he exclaimed. "I thought you'd be dead by now."

It took Nathan several seconds to recognize the captain. Then, diverting his eyes to the ground he muttered, "Sheriff Baker! . . . it's a surprise to see you out here."

"It's Captain Baker. My friends call me Tom, but you can call me Captain."

Nathan tried to ignore the insult. "I never figured you for a soldier."

"I joined up to fight in the Civil War and decided to stay when it was over. We've got real men in the army," the officer snapped. "Not cowards like some I know."

Shame burned into Nathan's face. Silently, he watched the officer and his men enter the store. The trader finished tallying up Nathan's furs and gave him a receipt. Nathan nodded, they shook hands, and Nathan said, "Here is a list of the staples I need. We'll see you in the morning." He appeared anxious to get away.

As Nathan and Tachechana mounted up, one of the women of the trading post walked from her cabin to the store. Nathan tipped his hat. Tachechana stared. *So that is what a white woman looks like,* she thought. The woman appeared unnerved by the Indian's penetrating green eyes and quickly ducked into the store.

Nathan led the way out through the gate.

"Goodbye, Miss Half-breed," said Crooked Nose.

Tachechana surprised him by using a trick she had taught Fox long ago. Slight pressure of her right knee to the horse's side made the horse step sideways. Fox knocked the guard down before Tachechana got her straightened out. It looked like an accident, but the horse, the girl, and Crooked Nose knew better.

As they rode out to where they would camp for the night, Tachechana asked, "How did that soldier know you?"

"He was the sheriff when my wife was killed. He hates my guts. His remarks turned the whole town against me."

They were still in sight of the trading post when Nathan

said, "We better camp here. If we go any farther we will be out of the neutral zone and fair game for any Yahoo that happens along."

They dismounted and built a small fire. Having brought no cooking utensils, they dined on jerky, pemmican, and parched corn.

After their supper they rolled out their bedrolls on opposite sides of the fire and sat staring into it. From the trading post came the sound of music.

"What is that?"

"A mouth organ."

"It's nice."

"Only if the one blowing on it knows how."

A coyote cry broke the spell. "That's what I call nice," said Nathan.

"I like that, too."

At last they crawled into their bedrolls and fell asleep. Nathan had his six-gun within easy reach, but he never needed it.

The next morning they were up at dawn. "We will eat at the trading post," Nathan told her. "The trader's wife will fix us a breakfast like you've never eaten."

Tachechana wondered if that was good or bad. Neither of the two guards at the gate spoke as the trapper and the girl rode past. Crooked Nose stepped back when he saw Fox coming through on his side, anger smoldering in his steel-gray eyes.

Nathan led Tachechana into the store, past piles of cloth and racks of clothing to the end of the building where there were four square tables with chairs. Nathan motioned for the girl to sit down and took a chair across the table from her.

Presently a tall woman in a long gray dress and white apron appeared. Her eyes were the exact color of her dress and her long pointed nose gave her a severe appearance. "Hello, Nathan," she said. "You know we don't serve Indians at the table."

"Her mother was as white as you are, Maggie, and she's my friend."

"Half-breed, Injun, all the same to me."

"She is my friend and we are going to eat here and now."

"All right," she muttered. "What'll you have?"

"You still have that cow?"

"Yep."

"We'll each have a full breakfast and a glass of milk. Coffee, too."

Tachechana stared after the woman. She was the tallest woman she had ever seen. "Is she a lady?"

"She'd like to think so. I guess she was one once, but living out here is enough to sour anyone."

"Why is she so tall?"

"The same reason you're so short. It's the way God made her."

"Do you blame everything on God?"

"I'm not blaming anything on anyone. It's just that she is tall and you are short."

"Which do you like better, tall women or short?"

Nathan was rescued by the reappearance of Maggie. She set a tall glass of milk in front of each of them and left without saying a word. Nathan bowed his head and prayed quietly for God's blessing on their food. At the "Amen" he picked up the glass of milk and sipped it as though it were a fine wine. The girl did, too. She was happily surprised at the sweet smooth taste of the cool liquid.

143

No sooner was the milk gone when Maggie returned with a platter for each of them. Bacon, three eggs, fried potatoes, and biscuits with honey. The girl was amazed at the ferocity with which Nathan attacked the food. She began a bit slower, but soon got caught up in the event as the various new tastes caressed her tongue. Even the coffee, which she didn't like, tasted better here than at the trapper's house.

Nathan pushed his chair back away from the table. "How did you like that?" he asked with a grin.

"Um!" said the girl as she stuffed the last of a honey covered biscuit in her mouth.

"Hope you still have the paper the trader gave you last night."

She reached for the deerskin pouch she kept tucked in her sash belt. "Yes."

"Good. Now we will go and trade for the things we need for the winter. The trader will tell you when you have used up all your furs."

"But they were your furs."

"You have done your share of work. It is the way of the white man to pay for work that is done for him."

"But I have only done what I wanted to do."

"And now I am doing what I want to do. I want you to have the furs."

"I have everything I need."

"I'll help you think of things."

Back inside the store, they came to a pile of blankets. Nathan said, "The fur room will be cold soon if you don't have another blanket."

She thought for a moment and began to look through

the blankets. Most of them were red and had black bars
across one end. Nathan explained that the bars were
trading marks. If the blanket had two wide bars and a
narrow one, it would take two and one-half beaver hides to
pay for it. He told her to take one with three wide bars.

She looked longingly at the shiny new hunting knives.
Hers was old and rusty. She picked one up and looked at
Nathan. He smiled and nodded. She put it on the counter
with the blanket.

She walked to the rack where there was a row of rifles
standing at attention. Both Nathan and Jim shook their
heads. Indians and half-breeds were not allowed to buy
guns.

Nathan steered the girl down the short aisle where the
ready-made dresses hung. There on the rack was a green
and white calico just her size. Nathan held it up in front of
her. Slowly she put her arm around the waist of the dress
and held it close to her. Her eyes sparkled. It was not a
squaw's dress, it was a lady's dress. Nathan put it on the
counter with her articles.

Next Tachechana picked out a pair of knee-high moccasin boots for winter, and some mittens. Nathan helped her
select a sheepskin lined coat and then picked one out for
himself. He couldn't talk her into getting a hat. She had
never worn one and was not about to start now.

"Does the trader have paper for me to write my words
on?" she asked.

"Jim, the lady needs a couple of writing tablets and
pencils."

"She can read and write?" Jim was amazed.

"She's learning."

"Humph! A half-breed Sioux that reads and writes. Never thought I'd see the day."

The trader indicated that she was about to run out of credit, so Nathan took her to a row of jars. Jim brought over a small sack and began filling it with an assortment of candies. Here she used up the last of her credit.

Nathan checked out the list of staples that he had given to Jim the night before, added a few items and the trader put them in sacks and boxes.

"You still have a lot of credit here, Nathan," Jim suggested. "I see yore still carrying that ol' cap 'n ball pistol. Let me show you a new handgun that uses the same .44 shells as your rifle."

He took the gun from behind the counter and handed it to Nathan. The feel and balance of the gun were perfect.

"I'll even take the old one in trade."

"No, I'll keep the old one, but I'll take this one and two extra boxes of shells."

"That's a lot of gun for someone who's afraid to use it," came a voice from behind them. Nathan turned to see Captain Baker and two of his sergeants.

Nathan tried to ignore them, but Tachechana turned to stare at the soldier. He was a big man, tall and wide, and he carried himself with a special air that made her uncomfortable.

"Why's your redskin staring at me, Cooper?"

"You're probably the first soldier she's ever seen," Nathan replied.

"If she was on the reservation like she should be, she would have seen many of us."

"If she was on the reservation like you think she should

be, she would probably have starved like so many of her tribe."

"Well, if they don't all get back on the reservation and respect the treaty of '68, General Custer will be here in the spring to see that there won't be any left to go back."

This conversation made the trader very nervous. "You still got 'bout two hundred dollars credit, Nathan," he said. "Anythin' else I can do for you?"

"Yes. I need a pack horse to get all this stuff back to my cabin."

"Hoss tradin' is whar I excel," smiled the trader.

"I'm well aware of that, but my Indian friend is sure to be a match for you."

As they walked out of the darkness of the store into the glitter of the bright late summer day, Nathan was clenching and unclenching his fists. He and Chana stood at the fence while the trader went inside the barn to drive the horses out for inspection.

Chana climbed up and sat on the top rail of the fence as the horses milled around below her. None of them pleased her.

"Are these the best that you have?" she asked in perfect English.

"These are the finest horses this side of the Mississippi," Jim began.

"Humph! The children of my village ride better horses than these."

"Humph!" returned Jim. Driving the horses back into the barn, he opened another door. Six sleek, spirited horses ran into the corral, heads and tails high.

"That's more like it," the girl said. She jumped down

into the corral and carefully examined each horse from one end to the other. She made them trot past her and watched their every move. She walked over to the fence and sat on the top rail again.

She pointed to a big bay mare. "That one," she said, slid off the fence and walked away.

Jim looked amazed, annoyed, and angry. "You gonna let that snip of a girl pick out a hoss for you?"

"Yep."

"That's the highest priced horse I own."

"Yep."

"It'll wipe your credit out."

"Yep."

Jim got a rope and caught the bay mare and led her to the hitching post.

While Nathan and Jim were getting all the supplies on the horses' backs, Tachechana wandered back into the store. To her surprise Crooked Nose was behind the counter instead of Maggie.

"Well, well. If it isn't Miss Half-breed," he said. "You're no lady. You're a no-good Indian half-breed." He was standing with both hands on the counter, leaning forward.

She walked up to him and stared straight into his eyes. Then she whipped her new knife from its sheath and drove it through the loose sleeve of his shirt, pinning it to the counter. When he reached for his gun, she grabbed his arm and with a quick twist, jerked him, face down on the counter. In a flash she had the knife point at his throat.

"Now, you will say, 'You are a lady.'"

There was silence. The point of the knife was pressed a little harder to the throat.

"You are a lady," he whispered.

"Louder!"

"You are a *lady*."

Nathan and Jim bounded through the door just in time to see Tachechana put her knife back in its sheath. Crooked Nose was glaring at her, red-faced, rubbing his throat.

"What's goin' on in here?" yelled Jim.

"Nothing," muttered Crooked Nose.

"Tachechana?" inquired Nathan.

"Nothing," she said with a wry smile.

Crooked Nose left the store.

"That one's bin trouble fer me ever since I hired 'im," Jim remarked.

"Maybe you ought to get rid of him," Nathan replied.

Nathan and Tachechana had mounted and were leading their new horse to the gate when Tachechana reined in. There, in front of them astride a fine pinto sat Swimming Otter.

"Is the daughter of Chief Great Bear well?" he asked.

"She is well. Is her father well?"

"He is well."

"Do not try to take the daughter of the Chief against her will," she said.

"I have one wife. That is enough."

"And the others?"

"All have returned to the village except Eagle Feather and Running Coyote."

"Will you tell them where I am?"

"No."

"I wish you to tell my father that I am well and with the trapper. I want no harm to come to the trapper. His traps are not to be stolen. He is a friend."

"I will tell your father the Chief."
"Go in peace, Swimming Otter."
"Go in peace, Tachechana."
Swimming Otter went on into the trading post and Nathan and Tachechana continued on their way. Nathan asked, "Can the word of Swimming Otter be trusted?"
"As well as my own."
"That's good enough for me."
The ride back to the cabin was uneventful.

Chapter

14

WHEN THEY WERE ALMOST TO THE CABIN Nathan pulled up his horse and listened. He heard nothing, but his insides quivered with his old companion, fear. After being away from the cabin for two days, he didn't want to ride up into a surprise.

They walked the horses slowly around the south hill and stopped as the cabin came into view. Both Nathan and Tachechana surveyed the area and the building. All appeared normal.

Just as they were about to remount, Nathan thought he saw a movement on the cliff to the north. He studied the area closely for a long moment. Convinced that it must have been an animal, he signaled the girl to move ahead. They rode the rest of the way up to the horse shed and began to unpack the horses.

Tachechana disappeared into her little room while Nathan built the fire and prepared the evening meal.

As the trapper placed the dishes on the table, he called Tachechana. Then he spooned up the food from the stove into their blue enameled bowls, looking impatiently at the blanket door. What was keeping the girl?

The curtain was pushed aside and Tachechana appeared. She had unbraided her hair and let it fall down over her shoulders. Instead of a deerskin shirt she now wore the green calico dress.

Nathan was speechless. Slowly he rose from his chair and walked over to the very self-conscious girl. The green of the dress highlighted the misty green of her eyes. The soft, feminine lines of her body startled him.

"You look lovely."

"Like a lady?"

"Very much like a lady."

He noted her shining hair, radiant face, and pretty dress, in contrast to the buckskin leggings sticking out from under the skirt. The lady needed undergarments, too. That would be remedied when he took his fall furs to the trader just before Christmas.

"Would the lady favor an old trapper with her company for dinner?" he asked as he extended his arm.

As she put her hand in the crook of his elbow and they walked to the table, she began to giggle. Nathan laughed.

Throughout the meal Nathan kept staring at the girl. The transformation in her touched him in a strange way, left him uneasy, even confused. Finally, he broke the silence. "What happened between you and the man at the trading post this morning?"

"He called me Miss Half-breed. I made him call me a lady."

"You also made him very angry."

"He made me angry."

"You will have to be very careful if you see him again. He can be a nasty man."

"What is 'nasty'?"

"Bad . . . evil."

"He will not be bad with my knife at his throat."

"You caught him by surprise today. The next time it could be different. Even though you are now a lady, to him you are like any other Indian."

Her eyes sparkled. "Do you really think I am a lady?"

"You are getting more so every day."

"Then I will wear my dress every day."

"The dress is not what makes you a lady. You must learn to be one even when you're wearing buckskins. But putting your knife at a man's throat is not being a lady."

"Was the woman I saw at the store a lady?"

"I don't know, I suppose so."

"Why was she afraid of me?"

"Because she didn't know you."

"If she knew me, would she love me?"

There was that word again. Nathan winced each time the girl used it. Whatever he said about love seemed to come out wrong.

"If she got to know you, I'm sure she would like you very much."

"But would she love me?"

"I don't know."

"You have gotten to know me. Do you love me?" She sat there with her green eyes burning into his soul. What could he say?

"Love is a very special word, Tachechana. It means different things to different people. Your idea of love and mine might not be the same."

"I do not know what love is," she interrupted.

"I know you don't, and I don't know how to tell you what it is. It is something you feel."

"Like hate?"

"Yes, love is the opposite of hate."

"I hated the one with the crooked nose today. I could have killed him, but you said that could not be done at the trading post."

"Can you tell me what 'hate' is?"

"No," she said. "But I can feel it right here." She placed her hand over her heart.

"As angry as your hatred made you feel, love will make you feel good."

"I feel good about Fox . . . and my father . . . and . . . you. Do I love you?"

"I'm sure in your way you do, and in the same way I love you."

With that she beamed and resumed eating. Nathan wondered if he had said the right thing. Surely her feelings were respect, friendship . . . the love for a friend. That was how he felt. At least that was the way he thought he felt. How else could a forty-two-year-old man feel about a girl twenty-four years younger?

Nathan got up from the table when he had finished eating and went to the bookshelf. He took down the writing tablet and pencil stub along with his Bible.

"Before I give you your new words tonight, I want to read to you from God's Word what He has to say about love." He turned in the Bible to John 3:16 and read:

> For God so loved the world that he gave his only begotten Son that whosoever believeth in him should not perish but have everlasting life.

Then he tried to explain to her how Jesus came to the earth to live and then die for those He loved.

The idea of voluntarily giving up one's life for someone else was hard for her to grasp. "If Jesus was the Son of the Great Sp—God, why did he not use his great power to kill all His enemies and live at peace with those He loved?"

"Because He loved all people."

"But they killed Him?"

"Yes. He loved them, but some hated Him."

"Then He should have killed them."

"That's not the way love works, Tachechana. When you love someone enough, you will even die for him."

Her face showed her surprise. "That is not the way of the Sioux."

"It is not the way of most white men either. It is the way of God. It is the way of love."

She shook her head in confusion.

"May I do my words now?"

Nathan's heart was heavy. "Yes," he said and took the pencil stub and wrote some new words for her to copy. Lady, dress, man, woman, and so on.

Instead of taking his pencil stub she produced one of those she got that morning from the trader. She attacked the words with her usual enthusiasm while Nathan went to the dirty dishes at the sink. Before he began washing them, he looked back at the girl. A lump came to his throat as he noticed how much more like a woman she seemed. In his clumsy way he loved her soul, and more than anything else he wanted her to become a Christian. In his clumsy way he loved her, too.

As he began doing odd jobs about the cabin, he could

see something was troubling her. Every once in a while she would stop writing and stare at the cabin wall. He wondered what she could be thinking, but chose not to interrupt her.

Nathan became so engrossed in cleaning and oiling his new gun that he didn't notice her leave the cabin. When he looked up and saw she was gone, he went to the door and pulled it open just as she was about to enter from the outside.

They were both startled. "I missed you," he said a bit self-consciously.

"I just went outside to sit and think for a while."

"You should have told me you were going. I would have gone with you."

"Sometimes it is good to be alone."

"Well . . . I was worried."

"Before I came to your cabin you did not worry about me."

"I did not know you then. You are my friend now."

Now Nathan saw the little girl before him. Not the warrior, nor the woman that wanted to be a lady, but a little girl who was homesick for her father, and confused by the new ideas and pressures that were being placed on her by her new friend. He wanted to hug her and let her know she was loved, but he was afraid to.

He put one arm around her shoulders and said, "Come in and we'll go over your words. I'll bet you got them all right again." They walked to the table together and sat opposite each other.

She seemed listless as Nathan went over the words on her paper and she didn't return his smile when he said,

"Just as I thought. Everything is correct." Then, seeing she was still sad he asked, "What's wrong?"

"I don't know. I should be happy. You have been good to me. I have a dress like a lady, but I am still just Tachechana."

"You will always be Tachechana."

"But your Bible says I should be different from what I am. I am a Sioux. But I am not a Sioux and I am not white. I am a . . . half-breed." There was despair in her voice.

"Are you ashamed of your mother?"

"No."

"Are you ashamed of your father?"

"No."

"Why are you ashamed of yourself then?"

"Because your Bible says I am evil."

"It says that I am evil, too."

"But you are not!"

"Yes, I am. As long as I live I'll be a sinful man. But Jesus came to this earth to give us the good news that if we believe in Him, we will go to heaven when we die. His death on the Cross paid for all man's evil."

Her face was still cloudy. "But it is better to live than to die. It is better to kill than be killed. It is better to be strong than to be weak."

"Jesus was strong, but He chose to die for us. He gave up His life for us."

"It is not the way of the Sioux."

With that she got up and went to her room. Troubled, Nathan went outside and sat down on a large stone, a place he was beginning to call his prayer rock. He used to just sit there and watch the day ebb away listening to the noises of the night creatures. Lately, he spent his time there talking to God.

For a long time he pondered the words he might use to get Tachechana to accept God's way of salvation. Why couldn't he make her understand?

Finally, Nathan looked up into the star cluttered sky. "Lord Jesus," he began, "I don't know why You brought this young girl into my life. I don't even know what I'm doing out here in the wilderness. But, Lord, since You have all the power of the universe, please don't let the sins of my past prevent her from coming to a belief in You."

Suddenly the heaviness was gone. Nathan felt a sense of peace. His tread was lighter as he walked down the trail to the cabin. The questions and doubts were all left up at the prayer rock. Quietly he opened the door, trying not to disturb the sleeping girl. To his surprise, she was sitting up waiting for him.

"I thought you would be asleep by now," he said.

"You were worried about me before because I am your friend. I was worried about you."

Nathan smiled. "Thank you."

"What are we going to do tomorrow?" she asked.

"If the hay is dry enough we must get it to the horse shed."

"The horses are crowded in there."

"Tomorrow we will build another fur shed and take all the traps and trapping equipment out. That will make room for the new mare."

She seemed relieved that the conversation had turned to less serious matters and went back to her room. After a last minute check around the cabin, Nathan blew out the lamp and crawled into his bed. All was still. After about five minutes the stillness was broken.

"Nathan?"

"Yes?"

"I love you."

"I—I love you, too."

"Goodnight, Nathan."

"Goodnight, Tachechana."

A lump came to the trapper's throat, and a satisfied warmth surged through him. He slept with a smile on his face.

Chapter
15

RUNNING COYOTE ASCENDED to his perch above Nathan's cabin long before the sun drove the sleep from the eyes of the cabin's inhabitants. He was growing impatient, even more impatient than usual. The dream of becoming Chief of the village of Great Bear spurred him on. He would soon have that horse and the girl under his control.

The wisp of smoke curling up from the chimney of the cabin told Running Coyote that they were up and about to start their new day. Perhaps today would be the day he would figure a way to capture the girl and her horse and gain the world he so desperately desired. If not today, tomorrow. His supplies were running low, but he would not return to the village of Great Bear without these trophies of his cunning.

Inside the cabin Nathan arose first and began the day by building a small cooking fire in the stove. Tachechana, a light sleeper, was awake as soon as he began to stir, but she lay in bed thinking of the events of the previous day, and the self-conscious admission to Nathan that she loved him. What she meant by that even she was not sure.

The rattle of the dishes was her signal to get out if she wanted to eat. Her hair was still down loose, but she was wearing her native shirt and breeches when she entered the main room of the cabin.

"Good morning, young lady."

"I'm not wearing my lady's dress."

"What you wear doesn't make you what you are. I wear buckskins, but you don't think I'm an Indian."

The girl giggled. "Your skin is white."

"And you are a young lady."

They sat down to eat and Nathan once again asked if she would like to thank God for their food.

"I don't know how."

"You know how to talk to me."

"You are not God."

"God listens the same as I do."

"He knows you and you know Him."

"He knows you, too."

The girl just bowed her head. Nathan asked the blessing on the food and they ate in silence. "We have two main jobs to do today," Nathan said. "The hay must be gathered and the deer you killed must be made into jerky."

"I have watched the squaws of my village make jerky," she said.

"Do you think you can get it started while I bring in the hay?"

"I will try."

"Good! We will start as soon as I wash the dishes.

The girl bounded to the buckets and out the door toward the river while Nathan gathered up the dishes and began his morning chores.

Running Coyote watched with interest as the girl left the cabin with the water buckets. His eyes followed every step she took on her way to the river. He noticed she kept her tomahawk and knife in her sash-belt. He noticed where she hung her garments as she took her swim. If there were some way to get the trapper away from the cabin at that time, he could catch her there when she was most vulnerable. How could he get rid of the Gray Head?

As he contemplated this action the door of the cabin opened and Nathan stepped out. Running Coyote remembered that each day, so far, the first thing that Nathan did was check the horses. Today was no exception. A plan was beginning to form. He watched the girl dress and bring the water back to the cabin. *Yes,* he half said to himself, with a growing smile.

After placing the buckets on the dry sink, Tachechana walked out to the horse shed. Nathan was taking a long-toothed rake out of the rafters. She was curious about the hay and how he was going to bring it to the shed.

"Build your fire and drying rack not far from where the deer is hanging," he said. "That way you can be cutting the meat while the fire is burning down."

She nodded and moved to the spot he had indicated, unsure of herself. After clearing an area about four by six feet of all grass and debris, she cut enough poles from nearby saplings to make a rack on which thin slices of meat from the deer could be hung.

The girl was determined to lash the rack together securely because she remembered one occasion when the wife of Swimming Otter had not done this. The rack had separated, dropping most of a deer into the fire. To compound her embarrassment, the wife was not watching the meat and it had all burned up. Swimming Otter beat his wife with a switch in front of the entire village that night. Tachechana decided that must never happen to her.

With the rack in place she built a small smoke fire in the center of it. Since the day was still, she constructed a small roof over the rack to prevent much of the smoke from escaping. Then she finished skinning the deer.

After the girl had sliced the meat into thin strips and hung them on the poles, she turned her attention to Nathan who was raking the loose hay into small neat piles. If you looked from east to west you would see a straight line of piles. If you looked from north to south, you would see straight lines.

Nathan was careful about things like that. She admired him for being so sure of himself. Was he right about her being a lady? Was he right in calling her an evil person as his Bible said? Should she believe in his Jesus so she could go to the white man's heaven?

Suddenly she was aware that Nathan was waving to her. "Can you help me gather the hay?" he asked.

"What can I do?"

"I'll fix a travois for the mare. You can lead her down the rows while I load the hay."

As she followed his instructions, Tachechana was surprised that Nathan could pick up an entire pile of hay with one flick of the fork. When the travois could hold no more hay, the trapper told her to lead the horse behind the shed. He took the hay from the travois in even bigger forkfulls than when he put it on.

While he unloaded the hay she ran to check the fire under the drying jerky. By the time she got back he was ready to go after another load. Most of the rest of the day they followed the same pattern.

When all the hay was stacked behind the horse shed, Nathan looked at the stack with pride. There was enough hay there to feed three horses all winter.

It would be his second winter in this cabin. Only once before had he spent more than one year at the same place. He wondered how much longer the beaver and fox would last. When they were gone so was his livelihood and he would have to move on to new trapping grounds. The thought of leaving this place saddened him. If he moved he would have to leave most of the cabin's furnishings behind. He had collected a wagonful of things since he built this cabin, and the recent fur-collecting season had made him prosperous. Not many trappers had two horses. Some had none.

He wondered to himself what would happen to the girl if he were forced to leave. The thought of leaving her put a heaviness on him that he could not think about. He enjoyed having someone to talk to . . . to care for . . . to care for him. But was he getting too attached to her?

The village of Great Bear was abuzz with excitement. The night before Eagle Feather had ridden dejectedly into camp with the announcement that he had given up his quest for Tachechana. He then went to the tepee of Great Bear to report that Tachechana was living in the cabin of the trapper.

Great Bear showed no emotion whatever at those words, but when Eagle Feather told him how Running Coyote had forced him to abandon his attempt to win Tachechana, the Chief was visibly upset. He asked if the trapper still lived at the cabin in front of the box canyon. Eagle Feather, surprised that Great Bear knew of the place, nodded.

Later that same day Swimming Otter raced into the village with the news that he had seen Tachechana and the trapper at the trading post. He had run his horse all the way to the village to pass this message to Great Bear. That night the Chief called his tribe together around a council fire to issue a decree that no harm was to come to the trapper.

While Nathan was thinking about supper, he noticed that Tachechana had gone back to scraping the last bits of meat and fat from the deerskin. He was surprised to see her soak the hair side of the skin with a mixture of water and ashes from the fire.

"Why are you doing that?" he asked.

"The ashes and water will make all the hair fall off in about three days."

"I knew the Indians had an easier way to do it, but I never knew what it was."

"That is why an Indian's buckskin is whiter than the buckskin white men make."

"You are becoming a good little squaw," said Nathan with a laugh, and ran for the cabin.

In mock anger she pulled out her tomahawk and began chasing him.

Nathan raced to the rear of the horse shed where he

grabbed a mound of fresh cut hay. As the girl ran around the corner of the shed he showered it upon her.

Tachechana squealed in delight, dropped her tomahawk, grabbed an armful of hay and tore after him.

He had run around the haystack twice before he realized the girl had disappeared. As he began looking for her, she came flying off the roof of the shed like a projectile, driving them both into the haystack.

For a long time Nathan lay there on his stomach in the hay while Tachechana, sitting on his back, pretended to scalp him. They both laughed until their sides hurt.

"Enough!" cried Nathan.

"Promise never to call me a squaw?"

"Yes."

She rolled off of him and they lay there a moment, giggling and looking up at the darkening sky. Nathan reached over and brushed some hay out of her hair, fighting off a sudden desire to caress her flushed face.

He climbed to his feet, then self-consciously he held out his hand and helped the girl up. They walked into the cabin hand in hand.

Supper was cooked and eaten. Words were given to the girl to learn, and Nathan again picked up a book to read. A review of Tachechana's new words and his walk to the prayer rock rounded out the evening's activities.

Nathan had only been asleep a short time when he heard Tachechana moaning. He tried to ignore it and go back to sleep when she cried, "No! No!"

He sprang into her room, revolver in hand, but she was alone and sitting up in her bed. As he lit the candle he saw fear in her eyes for the first time.

"What's the matter?" he asked as he sat on the bed beside her. She buried her head in his shoulder and shuddered.

"I had a bad dream," she said. "A mounted soldier was chasing me with his long knife and I could not find Fox. When he caught me I could see his face. It was Crooked Nose."

Nathan put his arms around the girl to comfort her. "It's all right," he said. "It was only a dream . . . a bad dream."

After a few moments Nathan asked, "Are you all right now? Can you go back to sleep?"

She raised her head from his shoulder and smiled a small smile. He released his hold on her and she sank back into her bed. As he tucked her blanket up around her chin she said, "I love you more than Fox or anything."

The Warrior, the Lady

Chapter

16

THE NEW DAY BROKE mellow and bright. Tachechana set the dishes on the table while Nathan cooked up a batch of pancakes in the heavy cast iron frying pan he called a spider. The Indian girl had been amazed to learn that a spider in English was an eight-legged bug. Most of the food Nathan prepared was cooked in his spider. She thought Nathan was teasing her when he told her the word was the same, but it had two meanings.

Prayer was said, breakfast was eaten, and Tachechana started to get the water. When she opened the door, she cried, "Nathan, the horses are loose!"

They both sped outside. The fence between the cabin and the shed was broken. At the edge of the brush near the trail to the river stood Fox. Rowdy was still standing in the corral, but the mare was gone. Tachechana surmised that the horse would try to go back to her old home at the trading post.

"Will you have any trouble catching Fox?" he asked.

"No, she will come if I call."

"Bring me my guns while I saddle Rowdy. Then you can fix the fence while I go after the mare."

"I'll go with you."

"No. You stay and take care of Fox and the other chores. The mare won't be traveling fast and I'll soon be back."

She went into the cabin and came out with Nathan's new revolver and his rifle, while he saddled Rowdy. He mounted his horse and headed south-southeast, following the fresh tracks of the mare.

Tachechana watched until he was out of sight. The fence had to be fixed but first there was time for a swim. She gathered up the buckets and walked down the trail to the river. When Fox saw her, she followed the girl to the beach and continued to graze as the girl undressed. She plunged into the water and noticed at once that it was colder than yesterday. Soon it would be too cold to swim.

With powerful strokes she quickly swam across the river, but the current took her about one hundred yards downstream. As she gained the opposite shore she began running back upstream to a spot where a rock ledge jutted into the river. From the ledge, about ten feet above the surface of the water, the girl dived out in a graceful arch and into the river for the swim back to her starting point.

The sun shone brightly on the patch of sand that was her private beach. She walked briskly back to the bush on which she had hung her clothes. After putting on her breeches and shirt she reached for her sash-belt and tomahawk. Surprised that her tomahawk had fallen several feet from where she thought she had placed it, she reached over and picked it up.

A rope noose snapped tightly around both her ankles and she was swept skyward in one quick motion, caught in a snare trap. Her own tomahawk had been the trigger.

Now she was staring into the upside-down smirking face of Running Coyote.

Without thinking she swung her tomahawk at his head, but had no coordination or accuracy hanging upside-down. In one motion he caught her by the wrist and his powerful hands pried the weapon from her grasp. He stepped back and looked at her.

"Now I have you, spoiled daughter of the Chief."

"You will never have me," she said, and swung at him with her fist. The action made her loose fitting shirt slide down toward her face, and she quickly pulled it up to cover herself. She was furious, but wondered why she was embarrassed. He had seen her naked before when the whole tribe would swim together. Why was it important to her now that she be covered?

"What are you going to do now?" she demanded. "You know I will never go back as your squaw."

"I have much time. How long do you think you can hang like that? You will soon see things differently."

"I will die before I will become your squaw."

"Then I will have your horse without you."

"My father would hunt you down and kill you."

"Your father could never catch me while I rode Fox."

"The trapper will come and kill you before I die."

"The trapper is many miles away. I have sent his horse back to the trading post."

"You will never have me."

"Time will tell," he said with a smile and stepped forward to pat the girl on the cheek.

When she spit in his face, he slapped her and grabbed a handful of her hair. "Soon the blood will rush to your head; you will lose consciousness and pass out and you will die."

"Then I will die as I have lived, a warrior."

"You are a fool!"

"Not so much a fool as to marry you."

"We will wait and see."

Already the rope was cutting into her ankles and her head was pounding from both anger and the unusual pressure of hanging there. Her arms were getting tired from holding her shirt in place. She would rest one arm at a time by letting it hang down, but the other hugged the shirt to her body. She would remain a lady to the end.

It was almost midday before Running Coyote spoke again. "You must be getting thirsty by now." With that he picked up one of her buckets and filled it at the river. He took a long satisfying drink and put the bucket full of water below the girl. "When you are ready to become my wife you may have something to drink."

"I will never become your wife."

"We shall see."

Tachechana's pain was intense. She had no feeling in her feet, but the rope had cut her ankles raw and blood was beginning to seep from under it. Her vision was turning red and blurred, but she would show no sign of pain.

Running Coyote was growing impatient. Nervously he ran his fingers along the scar on the side of his cheek and to the mangled ear. He walked over to where she hung and taunted her. She swung at him. He dodged the blow and slapped her face again and she swung at him again. He danced around her several times ducking the intended blows. He grabbed a big handful of her hair and tugged downward.

She could take it no longer and let out a scream of pain. Fox, grazing out of sight of the proceedings snapped up her head. The horse pranced into the opening where Running Coyote was still pulling down on the girl's hair, stretching her out between heaven and earth. The girl screamed again and the horse broke into a gallop. She was on Running Coyote before he could react.

Fox's shoulder caught him flush in the back and drove him to the ground past the girl. The horse reared up and came down with both feet on Running Coyote's stomach. Now it was the brave's turn to scream. The horse reared again and again, each time striking the helpless form of Running Coyote.

Finally the horse came to a wild-eyed stop. She stood there looking at the gruesome corpse at her feet. Satisfied that the task was complete, Fox stepped to where Tachechana hung.

The girl reached out with both arms and hugged the horse's neck. They were like that for several moments before Tachechana realized the ordeal was not yet over. What Running Coyote had said was true. If she did not get down soon she would die.

She locked her arms around the great horse's neck. "Pull!" she panted. "Pull!"

The horse responded until the girl thought she was going to be pulled apart. Her grip on the horse slipped and she sprang back to her upside-down position. Now she hurt more than before. The rope cut more deeply into her ankles. She could hardly see because of the pain.

The horse came back to her and she decided to try again. The horse responded to the commands again, but the girl's grasp slipped sooner this time than the first. It was no use. She was going to die, but hers would be the death of a warrior.

She thought it strange that she should die a warrior's death just when she was becoming a lady. Her father would be proud of her, but what would Nathan think? How would Nathan feel when he found her like this? Did it matter?

A new train of thought rushed into the stream of her consciousness. What would happen now? Would she die after dark and have to ride the Spirit World forever in darkness? What would happen to her since she was neither Indian nor white?

Fear of the unknown that verged on panic overwhelmed her. The one comforting thought was that she would die with her arms around the neck of her gallant horse.

She knew it was still early afternoon, but everything was getting dark. She no longer felt pain in her legs. They must be dead already, she thought. The sound of the river was getting farther and farther away. Then she could see nothing and she could hear nothing. She grasped the neck of Fox in one last hug, thought she heard distant thunder, then she was unconscious.

Nathan followed the mare's tracks for an hour before he caught sight of her. It was another hour before the runaway slowed down. Nathan meanwhile kept his pace with Rowdy. About noon he finally got a rope on the mare and headed back to the cabin at a fast trot, uneasy about leaving the girl so long.

As he came in from the south, he had a good view of the

grove where the action between Running Coyote and Tachechana had taken place. First, he saw Fox, with the girl's arms still around her neck. Shocked, he quietly edged closer and stopped, suddenly wary of a possible ambush. He slid from Rowdy's back and drew a trembling bead with his rifle on the rope holding Tachechana. The distant thunder she heard before passing out was the roar of Nathan's rifle. The rope parted and she toppled to the ground next to the body of Running Coyote.

Forgetting caution, Nathan ran up to help her, but Fox would not let him get close to the inert form on the ground. Not until Nathan got another rope, lassoed Fox, and tied her to a tree was he able to approach the unconscious girl.

She was still breathing. The bucket of water that Running Coyote used to torment her was nearby. He splashed some water from it on her face and cut the rope holding her feet together. Then he dipped his kerchief into the bucket and washed her face with it.

"Oh, God, don't let her die," Nathan prayed.

Carefully he picked up the torpid girl and carried her into the cabin, gently laying her on his own bed, and ran back to the river for the buckets of water. When he returned he wet the kerchief again and put it on her forehead. With another cloth he began to wash the angry rope burns on her ankles, leaving them exposed to the air. Once more he wet the kerchief and put it on her forehead.

When Fox whinnied down in the grove Nathan ran to the grove, untied her and led her and the other mare back to the horse shed. When he saw the fence was still not fixed, he knew Tachechana had been hanging in the snare for several hours.

He rushed back into the cabin after securing the horses to find that the girl had not stirred. Once more he wet the cloth and replaced it. He felt her bare feet. They were cold so he put a blanket over her. She still showed no sign of life other than her uneven breathing.

Walking back to the grove, he tried to figure out what had happened. The story was clear. The Indian had turned the horses loose to get rid of him, then, while Tachechana was swimming had set a trap for her. Fox had come to the girl's rescue and killed the Indian.

A horse snorted in the brush nearby. With gun in hand he walked toward the sound, not knowing what to expect. Through the brush he could see the brown and white markings of a pinto. Nathan advanced cautiously.

The horse was Running Coyote's, still tied where the Indian had left him that morning. What to do with it? The horse would not let him get close enough to untie it, but Nathan didn't want to leave the animal there all night with no water.

He returned to the cabin, hoping to see the girl better, but there was no change. After wetting the kerchief, he bathed Tachechana's head again, then made another trip to the river. On the way back he left one bucket where the Indian's horse could get a drink and carried the other into the cabin. The girl still had not moved.

At sundown, when he lit the coal oil lamp, he checked her ankles again. The swelling was going down and her feet were warm to touch. At least that part of her was improving. He covered her and re-wet the kerchief. Now there was nothing to do but wait; pray and wait.

Nathan took down his Bible, and opened it to Psalm 37

and began reading. "Trust in the Lord, and do good. . . . Delight thyself also in the Lord; and He shall give thee the desires of thine heart. Commit thy way unto the Lord; Trust also in Him; and He shall bring it to pass. . . . Rest in the Lord, and wait patiently for Him."

The Scriptures helped quiet Nathan's anxiety. The assurance that he had experienced the night before returned. The girl would be all right. He began to pray.

He was at the table, head still bowed when the girl opened her eyes. "Nathan?"

He sprang from the table to her bedside.

"Is it you, Nathan? Are we in heaven?"

"No, Chana. You are alive and will soon be well."

"Did you bring me here?"

"Yes, I found you in the snare."

"Fox killed Running Coyote."

"I know, I saw his body. I brought Fox up to the shed. She is fine."

"Did you scalp Running Coyote?"

The question shocked the trapper. "No," he said. "Did you want me to?"

The girl frowned. At last she said, "No, I am a lady, not a warrior."

"I will bury him tomorrow."

"His horse must be somewhere nearby."

"I've already found him and given him water, but he won't let me get close enough to untie him."

"Will you bury his horse with him?"

"Should a horse die because his owner was evil?"

"But what will he ride in the Spirit World?"

"Where he is going, he will need rc horse. Would you want me to kill Fox if you should die?"

179

"No."

"Then we will not kill Running Coyote's horse."

She nodded, then asked for a drink of water. Nathan propped her up and she drank the whole cupful he brought.

"Are you hungry?"

The girl hesitated. "My stomach is hungry, but I don't feel like eating."

"I'll take care of that," Nathan said as he went to the stove and started a fire.

He half-filled one of his pots with water and began cutting up jerky into small pieces. When the water began to boil he put the jerky in the water. He went to the small garden patch and pulled two carrots. After washing them he cut them into small pieces and put them in the pot, too. He added a little salt, a little pepper, and let it all simmer until the meat began to fall apart.

He ladled up a bowlful and carried it over to the bed, but the girl did not want to eat in bed. She tried to stand up, but tottered. Nathan helped her to the table.

She was sitting with her head bowed when Nathan sat down across from her. He prayed, thanking God for her recovery, and they ate. There would be no new words or reading tonight. As soon as she finished she went to her bed.

Chapter

17

When Nathan looked in on Tachechana the next morning, she was awake, a smile playing on her face.

"How do you feel?" he asked.

"I feel good except for two things, my head hurts and my legs are sore." She stuck her feet out for him to see. The rope burns were fiery red and in places had cracked open and bled.

"I have some salve that will help your ankles, but I'm afraid only time will help your headache. Can you walk to the table?"

She got up and with Nathan's help hobbled to the table. He took some black salve from a small round tin and gently rubbed it on the rope burns. When the wounds were well covered with salve, he wrapped them loosely with cotton strips.

Tachechana was amazed at the gentleness of the trapper. She doubted that a mother could be more tender with her child than he was with her. She was feeling so much better. Was it the salve or that Nathan was taking care of her so tenderly?

Nathan sliced the last of the bacon they had brought

from the trading post, fixed pancakes, and made coffee. When all was ready Nathan brought it to the table and sat down. He bowed his head to pray, but before he could begin, the girl's hand reached over and touched his. He looked into her green eyes as she said, "Thank you."

"For what?" he asked, embarrassed.

"For letting me stay here, for teaching me, for caring for me, for saving my life."

"Everyone needs someone to care for them," he said, self-consciously.

"Who cares for you, Nathan?"

"Why, I guess you do, and God does. He took care of you yesterday while I was gone. Maybe you should thank Him."

She bowed her head. Nathan had opened his mouth to pray when she said, "Thank you, God, for caring for us. Thank you for this food. Thank you for Nathan. Amen."

"Amen," said Nathan, but he didn't look up for several seconds. He had to blink away the tears that filled his eyes.

"After we eat you must lie down to help the pain in your head go away," he said. "I'll get the water today."

"Will you go swimming, too?" The grin on her face made Nathan redden slightly.

"I wouldn't tell you if I were."

She so much wanted to take her morning swim, but knew she could not. The pain in her head was still too great. Nor did she want to go past the body of Running Coyote.

Tachechana had moved all the dishes to the dry sink when Nathan returned. Firmly he helped her over to his bed and insisted she lie down in a place where he could keep an eye on her.

Tachechana felt small and insignificant in Nathan's large bed. It was fully twice the size of hers and seemed to be softer. She liked the way she could snuggle down into the mattress and pull the blanket up to her ears. It seemed she could feel Nathan's strength all around her as she watched the chores being done.

"I must go and bury Running Coyote's body now," Nathan said. "You try to sleep while I am gone."

"No," the girl almost shouted, and she sat up. "I must go too, and sing the death chant. Perhaps the Gre—God will favor him in the Spirit World."

"He does not deserve your prayers."

"He is Sioux. I am Sioux."

"Very well, but let me go dig the hole first. Then I will come and get you. We'll bury him together."

"Dig the hole so his feet point to the east," she said.

Nathan was shaking his head over Indian superstition as he left the cabin. From the shed he took a shovel and went to the clearing where the body lay. He noticed how thorough Fox had been in dispatching Running Coyote. It seemed as if every bone in his body was broken.

Nathan began to dig the grave, making sure that the deceased would lie with his feet toward the east. The earth was soft, but had many stones, some the size of a man's head. The trapper placed the earth on one side of the hole and the stones on the other. It was hard work.

The digging job completed, Nathan returned to the cabin for the girl. As she hobbled down the path, Tachechana asked to see Running Coyote's horse. When directed to the brush where the horse was hidden, she walked right up to the pinto and untied him. Together they walked to the gravesite.

Tachechana looked at the hole, then at the sun. Satisfied that all was well, she gathered together the blanket and weapons still on the horse, and the weapons Running Coyote had with him when he captured her.

Once the corpse was wrapped in the blanket and lowered into the hole, she placed Running Coyote's weapons beside the body and motioned for Nathan to cover body and weapons.

As Nathan began to fill the hole with dirt, Tachechana started the death chant. It was more of a wail than a chant. Once the hole was covered, Nathan placed stones one at a time over the grave. The last stone in place, the girl advanced and knelt beside the grave. She motioned for Nathan to do likewise.

Her chant changed its words and melody.

As she sang it in her high soprano voice, Nathan heard a nasal baritone join in very softly. He looked up into the face of Great Bear.

Tachechana must have known it was her father at the first note of his voice, for she did not look up from her prayer until the song was finished. Great Bear bowed his head along with his daughter.

The song came to an end, but no one moved. Then Great Bear rose to his feet. That was the signal Tachechana was awaiting. She rose and faced her father. He placed his hands on each of her shoulders and said, "Is my daughter well?"

"She is well. Is my father well?"

"He is well."

With that the girl leaped up and put her arms around his neck, and he hugged her around the waist.

Great Bear turned to Nathan and held up his right hand as a sign of peace. Nathan did the same. The Chief walked over to where Nathan stood and extended his right hand. Nathan reached out with his right hand and grasped the Chief's wrist. They both gave a tug downward and smiled at each other.

"Would the Great Chief of the Sioux join a white man in food?" Nathan asked in Sioux. Great Bear nodded and followed Nathan back toward the cabin.

As Tachechana limped over to the bed her father asked, "Did Running Coyote hurt you?"

"No," she lied, "he caught me in a snare, but Fox knocked him down and killed him."

"Let me see your feet."

She extended them for her father. "Nathan has treated the rope burns. I will be fine."

"Come here and sit up on the table." Nathan told her.

"I'm all right," she said but did as he ordered.

Nathan took off the bandages and studied the wounds. Most of the salve had either been absorbed by the skin or wiped off by the bandages. The sores were less inflamed.

"The white man's medicine is good," the Chief said.

While Nathan rubbed the affected area with salve and rebandaged the girl's ankles, the Chief told of the arrivals of Eagle Feather and Swimming Otter at the village. He told of the council fire that was held just the night before, and how he told the village that they must not hurt the trapper nor steal any more of his traps or furs. The trapper was to be treated as a brother of the Chief.

Nathan was deeply touched by the Chief's message. It meant he could even go visit the village any time he wanted. Tachechana was radiant.

185

"Will the Chief take his daughter back to the village with him, now?" Nathan asked.

Great Bear looked at the girl. "Does my daughter have a husband?"

She looked over at Nathan with a blush on her face. "No."

"Is she about to take a husband?"

Her gaze fell to the floor. "No."

"Has she learned the meaning of the white man's word 'love'?"

"She is learning," the girl replied.

"If she is learning, she must continue to learn."

Nathan could not repress a delighted smile. He would still have her for a while.

"You two must have much to talk about," Nathan said. "I'll fix us some food."

While he prepared the evening meal Tachechana told her father about the trip to the trading post. She even told him about owning a dress. At that the Chief grunted.

When Nathan began to put the dishes on the table, the girl disappeared into her room. After the food was on the table Nathan called her.

She made a grand entrance. Her hair was combed out and she wore her new dress. Nathan smiled as the Chief dropped the cup he had picked up. Great Bear stared in disbelief. In all his life he had seen only one woman as beautiful as his daughter, and that was her mother.

"You are as your mother was," he managed to say.

Nothing could have pleased the girl more. She tried to glide to the table the way the woman at the trading post glided into the store, but walking was still painful for her.

She sat on the stool as usual. Nathan honored the Chief with his bench and pulled out a box from the corner to sit on.

Great Bear was just about to start eating when Tachechana stopped him. "It is the white man's custom to thank the Great Spirit, God, before we eat." She bowed her head. When Nathan bowed his, the Chief did, too. Nathan prayed as best he could in the Sioux language, but the only way to end it was with an English, "Amen."

Tachechana rattled her dish when Nathan finished serving so her father would know he could begin eating. As the Chief and his daughter talked during the meal, Nathan watched them closely. He could tell her father was proud of his daughter and loved her deeply. If only he could better explain Christianity to them, show them how much they already practiced it.

The food was eaten. Nathan cleared the table, and still the two talked. She told her father of her first night there in the cabin and how she had scared Nathan. She told him of learning to speak English and to read and write. He told her of the new colt that was born to one of her favorite mares, and of the buffalo that were still being seen to the south. He then spoke of the white soldiers who were killing Indians and burning their villages to the ground.

"Several Chiefs of the Sioux want to make war on all whites," he continued. "Sitting Bull, Red Cloud, Spotted Tail, and Man Afraid of His Horses have all banded together to fight when the white soldiers come to Little Big Horn River."

"These are sad days," Nathan said. "Will Great Bear join them?"

"I have not decided, but already my brother, Little Bear, is preparing to join them."

"It will be a sad day for both Indian and white man," Nathan replied.

At last the hour came when all three of them felt the need for sleep. Nathan offered the Chief his bed saying he would sleep in the horse shed. The Chief would not hear of it.

"Never have I slept in a cabin. I will sleep outside under the stars."

Nathan knew better than to argue with the Chief. It didn't matter that this was Nathan's house nor that Nathan had fed him. When the Chief said a thing it was so.

Great Bear went outside to his horse, removed a blanket, walked to the drying rack that his daughter had made, and spread his blanket on the ground.

Tachechana, in the meantime, had gone to her room and changed from her dress to her shirt and breeches. She gathered up a blanket from her bed and hobbled out the door after her father.

They would spend the night together as they had so many times in the past. The two of them would watch the stars until they could see nothing in sleep.

Nathan found it strange to be alone. The girl had been with him only a few weeks. How he missed her even though he knew she was only a few paces from his door.

Strange, he thought, *how a snip of a girl can get under your skin. What will I do if she decides to go home with Great Bear?*

He blew out the light and crawled into his bed.

He was almost asleep when he heard the low murmur of Great Bear's voice quickly followed by the excited giggle of the girl. He wondered what the Chief had said to amuse her so.

He thought about Great Bear. The Chief was respected by folks at the trading post, a good man, a brave man. Nathan owed him his life. He added the Chief to his prayers that night.

Chapter

18

THE VOICES OF GREAT BEAR and Tachechana aroused Nathan from his sleep. They were singing the Sioux chant to the sunrise. Their voices blended in a pleasant yet discordant way, the girl's bell-clear soprano resonating with her father's nasal baritone.

Nathan looked out the crack in the door that was there for a rifle barrel. He saw them, sitting cross legged, straight backed, facing the sun that was just peeking over the horizon. He opened the door as quietly as he could and walked to them. The girl was sitting on her father's right, so Nathan assumed a similar posture on his left. He sat there until the Chief and girl had finished the chant, thinking how beautiful a way it was to start the day.

When the chant was complete, Great Bear said, "Is it the way of the white man to join in Indian ceremonies?"

"I believe the Great Spirit, as you call Him, and God are the same. As your song was to God, I may worship with you though I don't know the words of your song yet."

"You joined in the burial of Running Coyote. He was your enemy," continued the Chief.

"He was your enemy, too," joined in the girl. "He would try to become Chief if he had Fox."

"But he was Sioux as we are. The trapper is not even an Indian."

"He was a man," Nathan said.

"If all white men were as you, there would be peace on the prairie."

"If all Indians were as you, it would be a lasting peace," Nathan replied. "There is one way for Indians and whites to have peace. If they all trust in Jesus, God's Son."

After a long silence the Chief said, "Green Eyes, my wife, often spoke of this Jesus. He was a good man, but he let his enemies kill him. That is not the way of the Sioux."

"But since Jesus was God's Son, He did not stay dead. He came back to life."

"When a man is dead, it is finished," said the Chief, his hand slicing through the air.

Nathan saw for the first time one problem Indians had with Christianity: They could not understand the miracle of the Resurrection. How could he explain it?

"I'm hungry," said the girl.

"You are always hungry!" her father teased.

"Amen!" echoed Nathan, and they all went in the door laughing.

While Nathan fixed the morning meal of pancakes and coffee, Tachechana took her father and showed him her room and the things that Nathan had made for her and the things she traded for at the trading post. She showed him the papers she had been saving with her letters and words on them. The Chief was impressed.

Back in the main room of the cabin she showed him Nathan's books. She pointed to the Bible and said, "This Book is the Word of God." The Chief stepped back in awe and surprise.

"Can you read it?" he asked.

"Not yet. But I am learning."

Nathan interrupted. "She has many more words to learn before she will be able to read well. She is learning fast."

The Chief looked at Nathan and saw that he was bringing the food to the table. "Why does a man serve a woman?" he asked the girl.

She looked a bit ashamed, more at the rebuke than at not having helped Nathan. "Nathan has not asked for my help in cooking, but I get water, and help split firewood, and I made some jerky."

Her father smiled. "Did you let the meat fall into the fire?"

"No!" She was really getting embarrassed now.

"It is good. I would not want Nathan to have to spank you. I never could."

They all laughed as they went to the table to eat. Nathan didn't understand that Tachechana's embarrassment came from a secret between her and her father, that only a husband could strike his wife. Had he known, he probably would have been more embarrassed than the girl.

After Nathan asked God to bless the food and their day, the pancakes were passed and eaten.

"How long will the Chief honor us with his visit?" he asked.

"I must return to my village today."

"Why?" asked the girl.

"You know my children. If I am not there they will get into mischief."

Nathan frowned. He didn't know the Chief had children other than Tachechana. She saw the look on his face and giggled. "All the people of the village are called the children of the Chief," she explained.

After breakfast the Chief rolled his blanket and put it on his horse. "What will be done to the horse of Running Coyote?" he asked.

"It is a Sioux horse, used to battle and the hunt. It could be returned to the village of the Sioux," Nathan suggested.

"I have all the horses I need," the Chief said with a smug look.

"The horse could be given to Eagle Feather," the girl said shyly. "Since he cannot have Fox, he might as well have this horse. It is a good one."

Nathan looked the horse over closely for the first time. It was a good one. A horse like that would make any brave proud. He wondered, however, if Tachechana might not have a soft spot in her heart for the young brave.

"I will take it," said the Chief.

Nathan wanted them to be alone for their goodbyes, but could think of no gracious way to leave them. The girl stood in front of her father and looked up into his face. The Chief put his hands on her shoulders and said, "Learn the words and ways of the white man and teach them to your red brothers and sisters. Learn 'love.'"

With that Great Bear sprang up on the back of his horse. He took the lead rope of Running Coyote's horse and started out to the south at a fast trot. Just before he got to the edge of the trees, he stopped and looked back. He held his war lance high over his head and made his horse rear up.

The girl waved, and he was gone. She quietly walked into the cabin and got the water buckets. Her shoulders drooped as she limped toward the river.

Nathan watched her go until her form was hidden by the screen of brush. His heart ached for her, but he knew no words would make her feel better now. The best thing for her now was probably what she was doing, going for a swim in the cold water of the river.

As they ate their supper that evening, Tachechana broke a long period of silence. "How long will it be before I can read and write?"

"It will take many months. Tonight you will start to put words together on paper."

That seemed to brighten the girl's spirits and she finished her meal with considerably more enthusiasm. After the table had been cleared, Nathan drew on the top of her paper the letters: "My name is Chana. I am learning to read and write." She attacked the paper with her usual vigor. Soon she was showing her paper to Nathan.

"What does it say?" he asked.

"My name is Chana. I am learning to read and write." She was radiant when she realized that she was actually reading something she had written.

"You are learning very fast."

"You are a good teacher. But . . ."

"But what?"

"I still do not know what love is."

"Oh, Tachechana, there is no way that I can teach you love. It is a feeling that you must learn for yourself. I think you feel it, but you have not yet learned to put its name to it. What did you feel when you heard your father join in the death chant yesterday?"

"My heart was happy. It beat faster. I felt like singing something besides the death chant."

195

"That feeling was because you love your father."

"Then I have always loved my father."

"I'm sure that is true, and that he loves you and that he loved your mother."

"Who do you love, Nathan?"

Nathan got up and nervously walked to the stove and back. "I . . . love God and His Son, Jesus."

"Do you love any people?"

"The Bible tells us to love everyone."

"Then you must love me."

"Yes," Nathan admitted, "I love you."

"Why do you not take me for your wife?"

"I am too old for you. I love you the way your father loves you. You need a young man to love you as his wife."

"There must be different kinds of love then."

"Yes. That's what makes it so hard to understand."

The girl seemed satisfied, at least for the time being. She went to her room. Nathan went up to his prayer rock.

Somber thoughts troubled him. Was he falling in love with a girl young enough to be his daughter? It was absurd. Yet, she was the one who suggested that he take her for a wife. No, he could not be a lover to her, but he loved her.

He filled his prayer with her that night. For himself he only asked that God would give him wisdom to lead her correctly. When he found his way back to the cabin, it was already dark in the girl's room.

The next several days followed a similar routine. Chores, lessons, and a few special chores. The few hills of potatoes that Nathan had planted were dug and stored in a dirt

cellar under the cabin. Chana never knew there was a trap
door under the table to get there. They also carried in the
squash, and what was left of the carrots.

Each day it took Chana less and less time to get the water
from the river. Finally, one morning she arrived back at the
cabin totally dry.

"No swim today?"

"Too cold!"

"Well, summer always comes again."

On that day Nathan began to prepare for the new fur-
taking season. He and the girl went to the horse shed and
carried out all the number two and three traps that Nathan
owned. They checked each one to make sure the chains
were strong, the jaws lined up, and the pan and dog were
in good working condition.

Wanting to educate her further, Nathan took one of his
strongest number three traps and set it for her. He then
took a stick about one-half inch in diameter. With it he
sprang the trap and showed the girl the broken stick.

"It wouldn't do to get your fingers in there," he
cautioned. The girl somewhat loftily assured him she had
seen traps before, that many of the men in her village
possessed traps they had stolen from other trappers,
possibly even Nathan.

"Then maybe you'd like to come along tomorrow and
help?"

Her eyes lit up as they had not done since her father had
left. "Oh, yes!"

"We should kill another deer for fresh meat."

"This time you can make the kill." The impish grin made
Nathan smile.

Early the next day they mounted and rode north, crossed the stream where they had fished and started west. Completely by accident they stumbled upon the little clearing where Eagle Feather and later Running Coyote had made their camp.

Mice had gotten into a deerskin pouch of parched corn. Nathan noticed where a fox had jumped up on a large anthill to watch for a mouse. Foxes almost always jumped up on something in order to catch their prey.

Nathan took a narrow shovel-like tool from his saddle bag and dug into the top of the ant hill. He drove the stake that would secure the trap deep into the middle of it, coiled the chain around the stake and set the trap. Next he covered the pan with a cloth so dirt could not get under it and keep the trap from springing. With utmost care he sprinkled the trap with the dirt he had dug from the anthill. He finished the set by taking a small bit of vile-smelling bird entrail from a jar, and putting it about two feet from the anthill. He also took a switch of brush and wiped away his footprints from around the trap and bait.

The rest of the day followed the same pattern. They would ride until Nathan found a good place to set a trap. Sometimes it would be another anthill. Other times a scent post was set or a blind set in a trail. Sometimes he even built a small cubby out of rocks and bark. He would place the bait in the cubby and protect it with a trap in front of it. Foxes are smart creatures, but they are also very inquisitive.

At last the final trap was set for the day. The sun was still high so they rode south a ways to where deer were plentiful. Nathan wanted to show his guest how easy it was to kill a deer with a rifle.

They traveled about three miles before they saw the first deer, a big doe with twin fawns. Nathan shook his head. He only killed does in an emergency. Within a half hour they jumped a fat young buck. It bounded up the hill in front of them. Nathan waited. Just as he had expected, the deer stopped at the crest of the hill to look back.

Nathan's rifle spoke once. The deer disappeared over the hill. The girl looked with amazement. The distance from Nathan to the deer was almost two hundred yards.

Nathan climbed up on Rowdy and urged him up the hill. There, where the deer had been standing, was a large patch of deer hair and a few drops of blood. He followed the blood trail for about one hundred more yards and there lay the deer. It was dead before it even started down the far side of the hill. The girl was awed by the killing power of the white man's weapon.

The deer was field dressed to the Indian's satisfaction, even to the cremation of the parts that were not usable. Rowdy again objected to having the deer tied on his back so Tachechana had to hold him while Nathan secured the buck in place.

Back at the cabin the deer was hung to cool and drain in the same manner as the last one. Nathan headed for the river to find wild onions to go with the liver he planned to cook for the evening meal.

To get to one patch of onions a rocky ledge had to be crossed. As the trapper was crossing it, he saw something shining at the bottom of the rather deep hole. He got down on all fours to see what it might be. Every trapper was also a prospector, and some rich gold strikes had been found not too far away. He knew the water was too deep to reach the object, but he got as close to the water as he dared.

Then it happened. His right hand slipped off the ledge, and his entire body followed. It would have been comical except for one thing: Nathan couldn't swim.

"Help!" he yelled as his thrashing brought his head above the surface. "Help!"

The girl was riding her horse to the river to wash the blood from her hands when she heard the cry. She spun Fox around, then burned a hole in the wind to get to her benefactor and friend.

He was underwater when she arrived. Without a second thought she sprang from her horse and dived in. When she got to him, he grabbed her in panic. She could not pull him from the water nor could she get loose from his grasp.

Battling her way to the surface, she yelled, "Fox, come!"

Nathan's weight pulled her under again, but this time she let him drag her all the way to the bottom. With her feet planted firmly on solid ground, she pushed with all her might for the surface. Fox was in the water when they got there and Chana grabbed hold of her mane. "Pull!" she shouted. The horse responded and soon all three were up on shore.

Nathan coughed his thanks to the girl.

"Wouldn't you have done the same for me?"

"Yes."

Tachechana put on her dress for supper. Nathan, on the other hand, had only one other change of clothes—a store-bought suit for going to church. He felt embarrassed each time he put it on, but he had no choice so he took his suit to the outhouse and changed.

When he got back the girl was just coming out of her room. She took one look at him and began to laugh.

His hair was still plastered down from the soaking he got in the river and the white shirt and black suit made him look like a preacher. She could not stop laughing, even when she saw he was getting angry. She went to the shelf above the dry sink and produced the mirror. When Nathan saw himself, he had to chuckle, too. Then he took his gun cleaning rod and began chasing her around the table as she had done to him when he called her a squaw.

He finally caught her by the waist and they fell to the floor. Suddenly she was no longer running away and he was no longer chasing. They stopped laughing. He held on to her like he would never let her go.

In spite of himself, Nathan had fallen in love with Tachechana.

Love

Chapter
19

THE MELLOW DAYS OF SUMMER had quickly turned to the golden days of fall, and each day was a marvelous adventure for Tachechana as she and Nathan rode out to harvest the fur in their traps. All the traps Nathan owned were set now so they had to leave the cabin at first light in order to get back before dark. Nathan, realizing the days would continue growing shorter, pushed himself harder and harder.

The fur, plentiful again this year, kept the trapper busy far into the night as he pelted and stretched each hide. Tachechana insisted that she could help, but Nathan knew how badly she wanted to read and write. He only let her help with the fur after her lessons were complete. Even then he would try to add to her vocabulary as they worked.

Days changed into weeks and the shortened days brought colder temperatures and snow flurries. Nathan began to retrieve his farthermost traps and those sets that would be useless in the deepening snow. Finally the trap line was reduced to two dozen traps distributed in a circle around the cabin. Three to four hours was all it took to run the entire line.

It was a happy time for Nathan and his student. Now there was more time to read and write . . . yes, and even time simply to enjoy one another. The bond between them seemed to grow with every passing day.

It is a good life, Nathan mused as they were returning to the cabin late one afternoon. While he never pressed the matter, he was careful to always present the message of faith in God whenever the girl was sincerely interested. *God has His time and place,* he thought.

As they rounded the base of the hill nearest the cabin on that day, they were surprised to see six horses tied to the fence between the horse shed and the cabin. Four of the horses had packsaddles on with a large wooden box tied to each side. The other two horses wore riding saddles.

"They are Mr. Jim's horses from the trading post," Chana said.

"Yes. His best horses. Something is very wrong here."

Nathan, studying the horses, shed, and cabin, wondered who the riders were, and where they were from. He dismounted and motioned for Chana to take their horses out of sight.

As he watched in the gathering darkness, his visitors became active. First the smoke coming out of the chimney got thicker as fresh wood was put on the fire, then the small window glowed brightly as those inside lit the coal oil lamp.

Nathan scurried back to Chana and the horses. "I think there are two of them," he said. "You stay here until I call you. If something happens to me, you get on Fox and get back to your father's village just as fast as you can."

"I'll go to the cabin with you."

"No! You must stay here until I call," he insisted. "I'll find out what's going on in there."

Quietly Nathan clambered on Rowdy's back and slowly padded toward the cabin. He noticed he was perspiring even though the air was cold. His stomach felt as if it had no bottom, and he was annoyed at the accelerated beating of his heart. He stopped. Perhaps he should just go back to Chana and ride away. No! He had ridden away from trouble too many times already. The time had come to prove something to himself—"to be a real man" as Captain Baker had put it.

"Hello in the cabin!" he shouted.

A head was framed in the window for just a second, and a voice called out, "Come on in." It was the voice of the trading post guard—the one Tachechana named Crooked Nose; the one she had the nightmare about.

Nathan eased himself to the ground and walked behind Rowdy. Hidden from view of those in the cabin he drew his pistol, assured himself that it was fully loaded, and returned it to its holster. His hands were shaking, but he squared his shoulders and walked into the cabin as though he had visitors there every day.

Both of the guards were there. Crooked Nose was sitting at the table and his fat companion on the bed.

"What brings you boys out this way?" he asked and tried to smile.

"You might say we're here on business," replied Crooked Nose. The fat one laughed.

"I see you have some of your boss's stock tied up out there. Not like Jim to send his good horses into Indian territory," Nathan countered.

"Well, you might say we're in business for ourselves."

"That's what I figured," Nathan said. "I noticed those were gun and ammo boxes on the packhorses. You must be crazy to think of trading arms to the Indians." He walked across the room to the sink where the water bucket stood and took a long drink. Now he was in a better position to watch them both.

"The Indians will kill you and take those guns," Nathan continued.

"We made a deal with Crazy Horse for those guns. He'll live up to his word," said Crooked Nose.

"Just like he lived up to his word about staying on the reservation?"

"You let us worry about that!" Crooked Nose's voice was hard. "Where is that half-breed squaw of yours?"

"I told you before. She is not my squaw. She has gone back to her father." Fear began to gnaw again at the pit of Nathan's stomach. The events were falling into that same terrible scenario of years ago. His heart pounded.

"Don't lie to me, Cooper. I know she's around here somewhere. She made a fool of me once and I'm going to teach her a lesson she won't forget for a long, long time."

"I told you she went back to her father." Nathan's face was white. His hands were shaking and he could not swallow.

"She'd never leave here without this," said Fat One, holding up the girl's green dress.

"She would never wear that in an Indian camp," Nathan lied.

"Maybe not, but she wouldn't leave it here either," said Crooked Nose.

"I tell you she's not here!"

"You're lying."

"Why should I lie?" asked Nathan.

"To save your own skin. You're a coward and a liar. That army captain told us about you."

So it was out. Even here in the wilderness his cowardice was known. Shame overwhelmed him. Shame . . . and a sudden surge of anger. He knew he wouldn't give the girl up to them, but if he drew on them they would kill him and probably find the girl, too.

"Even if she was here, what makes you think I'd give her to you?" Nathan stalled.

"Like I said, you're a coward. We will have her one way or another."

His anger solidified, pushing away the last remnants of fear. And something began to happen inside him. An assurance that God was with him seeped into the core of his being.

"I won't let that happen." Nathan's voice was not squeezed off in his throat as it had been when he first came into the cabin. He noticed that his hands had nearly stopped shaking.

"Don't be a fool, Cooper. No half-breed injun is worth getting killed for," said Crooked Nose.

"Maybe I won't be the one getting killed." The words were no sooner out of Nathan's mouth when he saw Chana's face in the window.

Both men noted the look of surprise in Nathan's eyes, but only Fat One turned to see what had startled him. "There she is!" he whooped.

"Chana! Run!" Nathan yelled.

"Go get her!" Crooked Nose told Fat One.

"Move and you're dead," countered Nathan to the fat guard. The three men in the cabin were frozen for a split second. Then Chana bounded through the door, tomahawk in hand. Crooked Nose sprang to his feet and knocked her senseless with a vicious blow to the side of her head.

Now that the moment of truth had arrived Nathan's nerves were icy calm. All three men went for their guns. Crooked Nose, a bit off balance from his attack on Chana, drew his weapon first, but his aim was poor. The bullet splintered into the log wall to the left of Nathan's head. Nathan's gun spoke next, and his aim was true, the bullet smashing Crooked Nose in the center of the forehead, killing him instantly.

At the sound of the third shot Nathan felt a searing pain high in the left side of his chest and he was sent spinning by the impact. As he dropped to his knees, he fired once more at the blurred image of Fat One and passed out. The bullet rammed into Fat One where his breastbone met his neck. He was dying as he fell over backwards onto Nathan's bed.

Tachechana, still dazed from the blow she had received, crawled to where Nathan's inert form lay. "Please, God, don't let him be dead," she prayed. The rise and fall of his chest told her that, at least for now, her prayer was answered. Dragging herself to the dry sink, she pulled herself to her feet and wet a cloth to put on Nathan's head. He moved his head from side to side and moaned as she bathed his forehead. Finally his eyes fluttered open and he looked into her face.

"Are you all right?" he gasped.

"Yes," she smiled.

"The others?"

"They are both dead."

"Did they—hurt you?"

"No, I am fine and soon you will be, too."

Nathan looked at the hole in his chest and watched it first suck then blow air. "I'm dying," he said softly.

"No!" said the girl, fear now slicing into her as never before. "You cannot die."

"I'm lung shot," he said. "It's just a matter of time."

"No! You will not die. Crooked Nose was after me. I should be the one to die, not you."

"Do you remember when we talked about Jesus dying for us because He loved us?" Nathan's words were becoming more labored. "Tonight . . . I chose . . . to die . . . because I love you."

The full significance of his words welled up inside the girl and she sobbed. At last she knew what love was. She shared it with the man whose head she cradled in her arms. "You cannot die," she moaned.

"When I die . . . I will go to heaven," he gasped. "What about you?"

"I want to go to heaven, too, but I don't know if God wants me."

"His Book says, 'As many as received Him, to them gave He power to become the children of God. . . .' Do you receive . . . do you believe . . . in God?"

"Oh, yes, Nathan, yes!"

A smile flickered on Nathan's face, he coughed, and his head slumped down on his chest.

He is dead, she thought, anguish cutting through her. Then she noticed the hole in his chest still sucking and blowing, sucking and blowing. Tenderly she laid his head back on the floor and dashed out the door, running as fast as she could to where she had tied the horses. Untying both the horses, she sprang to Rowdy's back and galloped to the cabin.

Bounding back into the cabin with a rope she took from Rowdy's saddle, she quickly threw a loop around Fat One's feet. With no regard whatever for his body she tied the other end of the rope around Rowdy's saddle horn and dragged the dead outlaw from the house and onto the grass in front of it.

With great tenderness she eased the trapper across the room and lifted him onto the bed. Carefully she cut away a part of his buckskin shirt to expose the wound. From the box over the dry sink she took a clean cloth and cleaned the wound as best she could. Her eyes were mirrors of anguish as she looked into his face, wondering what else she could do to ease his pain and restore his health.

Glancing around the room, she saw the body of Crooked Nose and knew she had to get him out of there. Once again she put Rowdy to this task. Then, she took Rowdy and Fox to the river for a drink, brought them back, and turned them loose in the corral. Throughout the night she sat by Nathan's bed, wiping his hot face, stroking his head . . . praying that he would soon wake up.

As daylight began to assault the eastern sky the guards' horses, still tied to the fence, became restless. Chana knew they were hungry and thirsty, but she was loath to leave Nathan. At last she went out to see what could be done for them.

212

The packhorses had been standing all night with the heavy boxes lashed to their packsaddles. The boxes were too heavy for the girl to lower, so she loosened the ropes and let them fall to the ground. Then she removed the saddles, untied the horses and sprang to the back of one of them. Leading them all to the river she let them drink all they wanted and led them back to the west pasture where Nathan had cut the hay. They were safe there until she could figure out what to do with them.

Back inside the cabin Chana, feeling more lonely than she had ever felt, resumed her vigil over Nathan. *If only he would wake up,* she thought. *If only he could tell me again that he loves me, and I could tell him I love him, and that I do trust his Jesus.*

Into the night she watched him, never leaving him for longer than a few minutes. Several times he stirred and tried to wet his lips with his tongue. On each occasion she offered him water but he didn't seem to know she was there. Finally, fatigue got the better of her and she fell asleep sitting on the floor with her head on Nathan's bed.

She dreamed she was riding Fox with Nathan at her side. He was riding Rowdy and they both entered a dark forest. As they rode the day got darker and darker until they couldn't see each other. She called to Nathan in her dream, but he didn't answer. She called again to no avail.

Suddenly the day became brighter but she was all alone. She searched everywhere. Nathan could not be found. The day became dazzling white and it appeared she was riding into a spectacular sunrise. She called again and again for Nathan, but heard only the echo of her own voice. Then she heard a voice that sounded very much like that of her father, but it was speaking English. It seemed to radiate from the brightness before her.

"Tachechana," the voice said, "I am here to care for you."

She woke up cold. The fire had burned out while she slept and she had no blanket over her. A look at Nathan confirmed he was still breathing so she quickly got up and built a fire. The sun had already cleared the eastern horizon as she began the second day of her vigil.

Seating herself on Nathan's bed, she took his hand in hers. "God," she prayed, "Nathan has told me many times that you care for him . . . for us. He is badly hurt and I don't know what to do for him. Help us. Show me what to do . . . send someone who can help us."

Nathan stirred. The girl sprang to the sink for a cup of water. He swallowed a sip of the water and lapsed back into his coma.

Chapter
20

"HELLO IN THE CABIN!" A VOICE cried out, startling the nearly asleep Tachechana. It was early afternoon. She sprang to the door, snatching up Nathan's rifle on the way. Peeking through the rifle port she saw one of the soldiers she had seen at the trading post, a sergeant. Behind the sergeant were other soldiers hiding behind rocks and trees. She remembered what her father had told her about the army raiding Indian villages, killing everyone.

"What shall I do?" she wondered. "Will they kill me or will they help Nathan?"

"Hello in the cabin!" the sergeant called again.

"What do you want?"

"We're the army, ma'am. We've been trackin' two outlaws who stole guns and horses from the trading post. Tracked them here."

Both fear and relief surged through the girl's body. Slowly she put the rifle down and opened the door. Pointing to the two corpses in front of the cabin she said, "There are the men you want."

"Yes ma'am. We figured that might be the case. Are you all right?"

"I'm fine, but Nathan is hurt. Can you help him?"

"Yes, ma'am," the sergeant said. Turning in his saddle he shouted, "Send Doc up! We've got wounded here."

Several men from behind the line of soldiers mounted and galloped their horses up to the sergeant who joined them on their way to the cabin. Leading them into the cabin she pointed to Nathan's unconscious form.

The one called Doc said, "Get her out of here while we work on this man." As he and his orderly approached Nathan the sergeant gently took the girl by the arm and led her outside.

Captain Baker and several of his men were standing over the bodies of Crooked Nose and Fat One. When the captain saw Tachechana with the sergeant, he shouted, "Sergeant, get a burial detail and take care of those bodies." He turned to Tachechana. "Ma'am, can you tell me what happened here?"

"First I must see how Nathan is," the girl said nervously.

"There is nothing you can do for him until Doc comes out," the captain said as he led her away from the cabin and toward the horse shed. Reluctant to be far from Nathan, Chana stopped at the fence and looked into the corral where the horses stood pawing the ground.

"The horses have not been watered today," she said.

"Trooper!" the captain barked. "Take these horses down to the river for water. Sergeant! Have the men pitch camp in that grove of trees over there."

"Now ma'am, can you tell me what happened?"

The girl was surprised at how gentle the captain was. She was sure all soldiers were murderers and sadists, but here was an officer treating her like a lady. Perhaps there were good white men besides her Nathan. Hesitantly at first and, as the story unfolded, with more confidence she related the events up to the gunfight.

"Do you mean to tell me Nathan Cooper stood up to those two outlaws by himself?" the captain asked, shaking his head.

"Yes. The one with the crooked nose hit me when I went into the cabin," she said, showing the officer the bruise and swelling on the left side of her face. "I could do nothing to help him."

"That doesn't sound like the Nathan Cooper I used to know. . . ."

"People can change, Captain," the girl said.

"Cowards are cowards!"

"A coward wouldn't have stood up to those two," the girl said nodding toward the burial detail.

"I don't understand what could have changed him that much."

"It was God who changed him; He changed me, too."

"And how have you changed?" the officer asked.

"I was once a . . . an evil person, but now I am a Christian, and a lady."

Rendered speechless, the captain was staring at Tachechana as the one called Doc came out the door. His face was grave as he walked up to the girl and the officer.

"How is Nathan?" the girl asked.

Doc looked at the captain who just nodded. "Not very good, ma'am. The top of his lung was clipped, and he lost a lot of blood. There was only a little flesh holding the bullet in, in the back, so I took it out that way, but he is still in a coma. I've seen men survive worse, and I've seen them die from less. I've done all I can. I guess he's in the hands of the Almighty now—"

"The Almighty," the girl interrupted. "Do you mean God?"

"Yes," replied the doctor.

"Then Nathan will be all right. He and God are friends. May I go to him now?"

"Yes, but don't do anything to disturb him."

Hurrying back into the cabin, she noted Nathan's bloody, cut up shirt on the floor and that a large bandage had been placed on the wound. On the floor next to his shirt she saw the bloody bullet that Doc had removed. But most of all she noticed the whiteness of Nathan's tanned face. His beard looked darker than she remembered it. Reaching down to push his hair from his face, she noticed how hot he felt.

The doctor had walked in after her, but she didn't hear him enter. Startled, she jumped back when he said, "He is hot because of the infection in the wound. I cleaned it the best I could, but I don't know if he is strong enough to throw it."

"Is there nothing I can do?" she asked.

"Cool cloths on his head might help," Doc replied.

Chana jumped to the dry sink to wet some cloth, but found the buckets empty.

"Wait," said the doctor as she started for the door with the buckets. He opened the door and called, "Private! Get some water from the river for the lady."

"Yes, sir," came the reply.

Everyone is calling me a lady or treating me like one, she mused. *Nathan was right. I wish he could hear them call me a lady.*

In only a few moments there was a knock on the door. Chana opened it to find a young soldier with the water. She reached for the buckets, but the private insisted on carrying them to the dry sink for her.

Quickly the girl wet a cloth and applied it to Nathan's head.

"Is there anything else I can do for you, ma'am?" the young soldier asked.

She looked at him for the first time. He was standing next to the table, hat in hand. He could not have been any older than she was and his light blue eyes had a sobering look of innocence as they stared at her from under a thatching of yellow hair.

"No," she said, "but thank you for getting the water."

"My pleasure, ma'am." With that he turned and left.

How can such nice boys be the murderers of my people? she questioned. *There is still much for me to learn.*

As she sat on the edge of Nathan's bed she could hear the sounds of the various activities taking place outside the cabin walls. The day was about gone and she wondered how long the soldiers would stay. Another knock on the door stirred her from her reverie and ministration to Nathan. When she opened the door she was surprised to see Captain Baker standing there with two plates of food in his hands.

"Beg your pardon, ma'am," he said, "but I took the liberty to have the cook fix a plate for you. May I join you for dinner?"

"Yes, thank you," she answered, realizing for the first time she hadn't eaten in two days. "Put the dishes on the table and I'll get some bread out."

Before she got the bread she put water and coffee in the pot to boil. Bringing the bread to the table she said, "The bread is a little dry, but I'm sure it is better than your usual hardtack."

The captain smiled and said, "The men say that hardtack is good for throwing at grouse. If they scale it just right, they say, it'll cut the bird's head right off."

She smiled politely, but the officer could see that she was in no mood for humor.

"Nathan taught me to thank God for our food before we eat. Would you like to pray?"

"Ah, no ma'am. You go right ahead."

Chana bowed her head and prayed simply that God would bless the food and that He would help Nathan get better. At her "Amen" the captain looked up into her eyes.

"I surely don't understand what has happened out here. I never would have figured Cooper to do anything good. Why, if you knew what he did in the past—"

"I do know," the girl interrupted. "He has told me the whole story. What he was doesn't matter. What he is now is what counts."

"But how can a man change that much?"

"Nathan found out how weak he was. Then he found out how strong is his God. He has a way to get God's power. It is called prayer."

The captain smiled again and said, "Many things out here amaze me. First a coward becomes a hero, then an Indian girl preaches to me." With that he began to eat his stew. The girl ate everything on her plate and then drank a cup of coffee with the officer.

"My men found a new grave not far from here. Do you know anything about it?"

"It is the grave of Running Coyote," she said and related the story of his attempt to kidnap her and how her horse killed him. "Nathan buried him," she concluded.

With that she got up to re-wet the compress on Nathan's head. She took his hand in hers and wished for his eyes to open. They didn't. He just lay there, still as death itself. There was a knock on the door and without waiting for someone to open it, Doc walked in.

Chana stepped aside so the doctor could examine Nathan. She watched closely as he felt Nathan's head, and peeked under the bandage. He rolled Nathan's eyelid and gazed into his eye. She could make no sense of it at all.

"Get me a cup half-full of water," he said.

In an instant she was back with the water and watched as the doctor stirred a thick brown syrup into it.

"Whenever he stirs," the doctor explained, "I want you to try to get him to take this. Let him have as much as he wants. If he wakes up during the night call me. My tent is next to your door."

The girl nodded to the doctor appreciatively and he and the captain left. She resumed her watchful vigil from her usual spot on the edge of Nathan's bed. The sounds of the camp grew quieter until she could hear only her own breathing and Nathan's. Still she sat there, nodding when she could no longer remain awake, but never so asleep as not to hear Nathan if he stirred.

Twice during the night he did stir, and each time she was able to get a little of the medicine into him. Once he took a spoonful and once he took two before he lapsed back into his coma. Chana was sure he didn't even know she was there. *If only I could make him know how much I love him,* she thought.

The next morning Doc came to check on Nathan while the rest of the troop broke camp. He said there was no change in the trapper's condition and nodded approvingly when Chana reported she had gotten him to take three spoonfuls of medicine. Showing her how to mix a fresh supply of the medicine he told her to get as much as she could into Nathan, up to a cup a day.

The soldiers had mounted and were about to depart when the captain came into the cabin.

"Is there anything we can do to help you?" he asked the girl.

"No," she replied.

"I asked Doc about taking you and Cooper back to the trading post, but he said the trip would be too hard on him."

"I think Nathan would want to stay here," she said. "I am not a doctor, but I will care for him with the medicine Doc left."

"Do you have enough food here?"

"Yes."

"Then my men and I will be going. I'll have a patrol stop by whenever there is one in the area. Good luck and goodbye."

"Goodbye. Thank you."

A new surge of loneliness swept over the girl as the soldiers rode away. Yet, she was glad to be rid of them in one way. Now she would be able to devote all her time and energy to the care of Nathan, who needed her so badly.

She felt his head. Finding it fevered she applied the cold wet cloths and spoke gently to him though he could not hear her. In the stillness she wondered at the sound of her own voice. Never before had she actually listened to the musical quality of the English language. Compared to the rough guttural sounds of the Sioux it was smooth and . . . ladylike. A tear rolled down her cheek, but she was not ashamed of it. *A lady should weep for her man,* she thought.

One day melted into another . . . until a week had passed. Several times each day Nathan would stir enough to take a spoonful or two of Doc's medicine. Usually by nightfall he would take the entire cupful Doc had prescribed. When the entire cup was emptied in the morning, Chana made a broth for him in the afternoon. It was the same jerky, carrot, and water combination he had used when she was recovering from her encounter with Running Coyote.

It was early in the second week when the trapper's cabin received a visit from the soldiers. They told the girl it was a standard patrol, but on the way they had killed a deer so Chana would have fresh meat. They also brought some supplies from the trading post at Captain Baker's suggestion, and more medicine from Doc.

A warm feeling flooded her as she realized that she was accepted by the white people as a person. She no longer felt that she was neither red nor white: She was both red and white! By her courage and daring she had been accepted as an Indian, and by her courage and ladylike manner she was accepted as a white. *And I owe it all to Nathan,* she thought.

Again the mood of loneliness overtook her after the soldiers left. By the end of the second week of Nathan's convalescence she was beginning to despair for his life. For the first time she permitted herself the thought that he might not live.

"What will I do if he should die?" she asked herself. "I'm not ready to enter the white man's world yet, and I'm no longer the Indian I once was."

Then Nathan stirred. Quickly the girl spooned the medicine into his mouth . . . he coughed . . . and slumped back into unconsciousness. She noticed how thin Nathan had become. *How long can he live without eating?* she wondered.

The strain and fatigue of the ordeal suddenly overwhelmed her and she wept openly and unashamedly.

So black was her mood that she left Nathan's bedside and sat at his place at the table where she could look across the room at him. After a few moments she returned to his bed, held his hand and wept again. The tears she had suppressed for her lifetime were finally released and she cried as if she would never stop.

As she sat there, her body convulsing with sobs, she remembered the dream she had about losing Nathan in the dark forest and the voice that spoke to her out of the brightness. It said, "Tachechana, I am here to care for you."

"God," she prayed out loud, "was it You who spoke to me in the dream? I need You to care for me and for Nathan. He is hurt so bad, and if he doesn't eat soon, he will die. I know if he dies he will go to Your heaven. He would like that. But God, I love him. And I need him *here. . . .*"

Nathan's eyelids flickered open. For the first time he looked directly at her. A smile spread across his wan face. The light was back in his eyes.

"Chana . . . Chana . . . I am here. I love you. And I am going to live."

ABOUT THE AUTHOR

JACK METZLER brings to Serenade not only a beautiful love story based on research in the Black Hills of South Dakota, but a unique perspective: that of a male author. His writing skills and sensitive touch with the characters and wilderness setting combine to make *Tachechana* an important addition to the Serenade line.

Jack and his family live in Michigan.